"I think I want to get to know you, Jade. Maybe very well. Does that sound like something that would interest you?"

She turned toward Byron and looked up into his face. "You confuse me. Yes, it would interest me. It might even interest me a lot. But there are things we'd have to get straight first."

"Such as?"

"I'm not in the market for a casual lover."

Just like that. Byron recovered fast. "Casual lovers aren't my thing either."

"There's something more important than that."

"Fire away."

"I—" Abruptly, she swung away and stood with her back to him.

"You what?" Her moods swept back and forth. "Jade, what is it?"

"I don't like this. I don't like it one bit."

"Okay," Byron said. He moved beside her. "Would you please tell me what it is? I can take it, I assure you."

Even in the darkness he could see anxiety in her eyes. "I've got to know why you're following Ian Spring around . . ."

BOOK YOUR PLACE ON OUR WEBSITE AND MAKE THE READING CONNECTION!

We've created a customized website just for our very special readers, where you can get the inside scoop on everything that's going on with Zebra, Pinnacle and Kensington books.

When you come online, you'll have the exciting opportunity to:

- View covers of upcoming books
- Read sample chapters
- Learn about our future publishing schedule (listed by publication month *and author*)
- Find out when your favorite authors will be visiting a city near you
- Search for and order backlist books from our online catalog
- Check out author bios and background information
- Send e-mail to your favorite authors
- Meet the Kensington staff online
- Join us in weekly chats with authors, readers and other guests
- Get writing guidelines
- AND MUCH MORE!

Visit our website at
http://www.kensingtonbooks.com

FINDING IAN

Stella Cameron

ZEBRA BOOKS
KENSINGTON PUBLISHING CORP.
http://www.kensingtonbooks.com

ZEBRA BOOKS are published by

Kensington Publishing Corp.
850 Third Avenue
New York, NY 10022

All Kensington titles, imprints and distributed lines are available at special quality discounts for bulk purchases for sales promotion, premiums, fund-raising, educational or institutional use.

Special book excerpts or customized printings can also be created to fit specific needs. For details, write or phone the office of the Kensington Special Sales Manager: Kensington Publishing Corp., 850 Third Avenue, New York, NY 10022. Attn. Special Sales Department. Phone: 1-800-221-2647.

Zebra and the Z logo Reg. U.S. Pat. & TM Off.

First Hardcover Printing: January 2001
First Paperback Printing: February, 2002
10 9 8 7 6 5 4 3 2 1

Printed in the United States of America

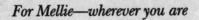

For Mellie—wherever you are

Chapter One

One shoe box with a broken lid. One lousy shoe box held together by a knotted length of graying elastic.

Byron saw the end of the thing beneath a pile of shirts he never wore. He'd probably have thrown them out years ago—only somewhere inside him where he tried never to look hovered a warning not to go near that pile.

Ignoring the deluge of falling clothes, he pulled the box from a shelf in the walk-in closet, carried it to the bedroom, and dropped it on the bed.

It slipped to the floor. The elastic snapped.

The life of Byron and Lori Frazer spilled out. Two years of loving scattered on a green and rust Chinese silk rug Lori never saw. Loving, and hoping, and praying, and daring to laugh—and losing. Thirteen years ago they'd lost the battle for a future together, and it hurt all over again, dammit, it hurt almost as much this morning as it had hurt then.

He went to twenty-foot-high windows overlooking a sheer drop to San Francisco Bay. Here, high up on the west side of Tiburon, he'd managed to find a kind of peace, a kind of insulation from the demands of his life that he'd rather leave either in his consulting rooms in the city, or at the TV station where he spent hours every day.

Jim Wade, the private investigator who'd worked for him for years, had obviously followed Byron's offhand invitation to finish his coffee—even though Byron had excused himself from their meeting to come up here. While Byron watched, Wade slowly emerged from the two-story house and sauntered to his inconspicuous brown Honda.

An inconspicuous car for an inconspicuous man who made his living watching, while not being watched. And he was good at it. Jim Wade was the perfect, unremarkable face in any crowd.

He glanced toward a cloudless blue sky, and the water that shimmered beneath an early March sun. Blue, on blue, on blue. Shaded bowls of blue, their rims dissolving into each other. Bougainvillaea in colors of ripe oranges, red, and a luminous purple billowed over white stucco walls edging the steep cliffs. The twisted limbs of stunted pines backed the wall and made jigsaw pieces of the horizon.

Wade threw a battered black briefcase and the jacket of his brown and beige striped seersucker suit into the Honda, climbed in, and drove away from the parking area at the back of the house.

Then he was gone.

Wade was gone, and Byron was left with no one but himself to make the decisions he'd hoped would never have to be made. Not that the fault for what had happened could be set at anyone's feet but his own. And he could choose to walk away from responsibility. After all, he'd turned his back on responsibility once before and been able to convince himself that what he'd done was for the best—for all concerned. And it might have been, mightn't it?

He returned to the side of the bed and went to his knees. He started gathering pieces of paper and photographs. Notes. Pressed flowers that crumbled at the slightest touch. A bracelet of colored yarn—faded now—and with Lori's name, in turquoise-colored beads, woven into the strands. Cards, Lori's, and even some of Byron's, handmade. They'd had so little money, not that he could have felt for a store-bought card what he'd felt for each of Lori's simple designs, or her words that could not have been for anyone but him. "I promise I'll never slow you down. I'll only be free if you're free. Be free, Byron. Love you, Lori."

He hadn't wanted to be free, not free of Lori, the sweetest, most honest creature ever to be part of his life.

He had owed her so much, but he'd failed her. And when he'd failed her, he'd failed himself. He had turned her concern for him into an excuse to do what he'd wanted to do—to avoid anything that might tie him down.

Hell, he didn't know anymore. He hadn't known then, but after all he'd been doing what Lori told him to do—choosing freedom at a time when to do anything else would make his way not just hard, but near impossible.

Byron Frazer had betrayed his wife.

The box should have stayed where it was.

A picture taken in Golden Gate Park. Lori clowning by a tree trunk. An insubstantial girl, with long, fine blond hair blowing away from her face, a bright grin, and gray eyes screwed up against the sun. He'd been playing his guitar and she'd leaped up to dance. She'd twirled and laughed, twirled and laughed, and he abandoned the guitar for their old point-and-shoot camera. Her slender body and well-shaped legs showed in shadow through a thin, flower-strewn, gauze dress.

His hands shook.

"Byron! Byron, are you here?" The unmistakable voice of his agent, Celeste Daily, came from the foyer. Celeste had her own key and never hesitated to use it. "Byron, darling, it's me, Celeste."

He listened to her inevitable exceedingly high heels clip on the terra-cotta tiles that covered the ground floor. She would be checking each room for him.

Celeste, his agent, and the woman who thought she owned him.

Tucking the photo of Lori into his shirt pocket, he made a rapid pile of everything else, and crammed it into the box. Then he pushed the box under the bed.

Celeste was already climbing the stairs.

What the hell was he going to do?

"Byron Frazer? Come out, come out. Be warned, I'm comin' in if you don't come out."

Some might be beguiled by her playfulness. Byron knew her too well.

The bedroom door stood open to a wide balcony that ran around the second floor. This room, decorated for him by the strangers he'd hired to make the house peaceful—his only instruction to them—echoed the cool greens and creams, and soft white used in the foyer that soared to open beams above the upper floor.

Tall, slender, elegant in putty-colored silk, her blond hair curving smoothly to chin level, Celeste appeared on the threshold. She looked at him, and frowned. "Byron? Honey, what gives? There's a studio full of people twiddling their thumbs and waiting for you over there." She looked at the phone by the bed, took obvious note of the unplugged cord.

He could lie, say he was sick, had unplugged the phone to get some rest, then overslept. Only this wasn't a time for lies. He shifted his foot slightly, and the toe of his right sneaker made contact with the shoe box.

No more lying, especially not to himself.

"For God's sake, what is it?" Celeste jiggled the car keys she held in one hand. "Oh, there isn't time now. We'll talk about it while we drive. I met Rachel outside, by the way. She's not a happy camper. She likes early morning visitors less than you do. Good housekeepers are hard to come by— you'd better smooth her feathers."

"Rachel's fine. She enjoys complaining."

He didn't have to deal with what Jim Wade had told him. For thirteen years he'd avoided doing anything—why start now? He crossed his arms and felt the photo in his pocket.

The coldness, the old coldness he'd learned to ignore, spread beneath his skin. His scalp tightened and he felt himself growing distant. Celeste's mouth moved. He watched, even shook his head a little and turned away as if dismissing her, but he couldn't hear her clearly anymore.

He drew a deep, deep breath and closed his eyes, willing himself to be calm, to stop himself from moving away, moving inside himself. It was Byron the quitter who ran away. He wasn't that man anymore. He wouldn't run again. Would he?

"Why didn't you come to the studio?" Celeste asked. "Or at least call and say you'd be late."

He struggled to concentrate. People thought him rude, arrogant, when he turned his silence on them, but he literally withdrew, just as his mother had withdrawn from his father's mental and physical battering. In the end she had gone so far away she'd never returned . . .

"Byron?"

"We're well ahead of schedule on the tapings," he said.

"That doesn't matter. You can't leave that many people standing around doing nothing just because you decide to sleep in. That's expensive. And it's not your style. You can't—"

"How do you know what my style is?" Much as he yearned to shout, he kept his voice steady. His father had been a screamer and Byron had learned to stuff down any urge to follow in good old dad's footsteps. "You don't know me, Celeste."

Her large, violet-colored eyes grew hard. "If you say so. That's a discussion that'll have to wait. Right now I need you downstairs in my car. We've got some major opportunities lining up. You're one hell of a success. I do know that about you. You're thirty-four, and you're already a media phenomenon. Dr. Byron Frazer, the country's leading popular expert on the family—and every woman's ideal man. Let's go."

"You go," he said. "I've got some things to attend to. Be a love and go buy me time, hm?" He managed a smile. The instant softening in her perfect features brought him no pleasure. So he had a face and smile that had women eating out of his hands. Big deal. They wouldn't want to come within miles if they knew what he really was. No woman worth knowing would want to.

"Byron, please—"

"I just told you I've got things to do."

"You bet you do. If we hurry, we'll at least make lunch. Buddy's talking about product tie-ins."

"We've already got product tie-ins."

"Other than tapes and videos and books."

Byron rubbed his eyes. "I'm not talking about this now."

"Because of the detective?"

He grew still, then slowly dropped his hands. "What did you say?"

Celeste walked across his bedroom to the simple teak writing table by the windows. She skirted the table and sat atop deep green corduroy cushions on a long window seat. "Rachel was outside deadheading some flowers. Your Mr. Wade was just leaving."

"*My* Mr. Wade . . . How do you know his name?"

"He stopped and said goodbye to Rachel, and she said, 'Goodbye, Mr. Wade.' Then Rachel rolled her eyes at me and said, 'Detectives wanting coffee almost before my eyes are open.' " Celeste crossed one long leg over the other and didn't attempt to stop her skirts from slipping up her thighs.

"What's happened, Byron? Why would the police be here?"

"He's not a policeman. He's a private investigator—and my business with him is private."

She raised her silver-blond brows, got up, and bent over the writing table.

Damn, he'd forgotten about the papers Wade had brought and left spread out.

Celeste picked up a photograph and studied it. "Who's this?"

"No one you know." No one he knew—he'd made sure of that.

On that terrible day he was never going to forget, Lori had said, *"Byron, promise me you'll put this behind you if something goes wrong. Promise me you won't let anything stop you from doing what you want to do."*

"This is what I want to do," he told her.

"But if . . . if something doesn't turn out the way we hope? You won't be stupid, will you? You won't give it all up. We both know that would never work. You wouldn't be able to manage everything."

"No, Lori, we don't both know that. You think you do. But nothing's going wrong."

"Promise me, please," Lori said. *"You're going to be a great psychologist. You're going to help people like us. Like the people we were when we were kids."*

"I promise you I'm always going to try to do what's right."

But afterward he'd lost his nerve.

* * *

"Nice-looking kid," Celeste said, and tossed the photograph down again. "C'mon, open up to me. What's going on?"

"Back off, Celeste."

"We've been through too much together for me to shrivel up just because you sound pissed."

"I've got to leave California for a while. Maybe quite a while." That had been the last thing he'd intended to say. But that was the answer, that's what he had to do—what was right. Finally. The pressure on his chest lightened. He'd made his decision. "Yeah, that's it. I'm going away. We've got plenty in the can at the station. If necessary they can go to reruns."

"That's the craziest suggestion you've ever made." She hurried around the table and came to him, grasped his biceps. "You're tired, that's all. Everything's gone so fast and you haven't had a real break in two years. Take a vacation. Go to Grand Cayman for a couple of weeks. You like it there."

"I don't like it there. I'm going to . . ." No, he would not tell her or anyone else where he was going. "I'm going to visit someone."

"Who?"

She never backed off, never gave up.

"My son," he told her, meeting her eyes while, inside, he began to move away again. The faint, familiar buzzing began at the center of his mind. The palms of his hands sweated—cold sweat.

Celeste dropped her hands. "*Son?* What son? You don't have—you *can't* have a son, for God's sake. What are you saying to me?" Her voice rose to a thin shriek.

"I have a son," he said, and this time the sound of it felt more real.

"No. Where is he? With his mother?"

"I'm not talking about Lori."

"Oh, my, God." Clapping her hands over her mouth, she tottered to the bed and sat down with a thump. "Lori? We've known each other for years. We've been more than business partners, Byron. But now there's a son, and *Lori?*"

"I've told you I won't talk about Lori. I've got a son who needs me." A son who might or might not need him, but Byron intended to find out for sure.

"That's him." She nodded toward the table. "The blond kid with the dog. I don't get it. How could you do this? Dr. Frazer can't have a secret kid stashed away somewhere. Or a wife, or ex-wife, or whatever. Think what that could do to your credibility. If you'd been straight about it up front, we could have made sure there was never any mess to clean up."

A mess to clean up? "Please go . . . Celeste, please give me some space. This isn't something I can talk about with you. Not with anyone. I need—"

"Oh, Byron." She surged to her feet and rushed to him, wrapped her arms around him. "I'm sorry, I'm sorry. Forgive me, please. I don't know . . . You shocked me and I've never been good at shocks. Why aren't I saying what I should be saying. This is *wonderful.* You have a son and he's beautiful. He must get the blond hair from his mother, but I bet he's got your eyes. What a beautiful boy."

"You can hardly see him in that picture. He's too far away." Wade had been warned never to intrude on Ian, to make certain the boy was never frightened.

"I don't have to see him any clearer to know he's wonderful. He's your boy. He'd have to be wonderful. A green-eyed blond. He'll soon be fighting off the girls. I want to meet him. I want to come with you."

There was only one person he'd like with him when—if—he met Ian, and she wouldn't be available. "No." He stiffened and gently disentangled himself from her. Forcing a smile, he said, "But thank you. Cover for me here, will you? Family is what I'm supposed to be about. You can say—without lying—that I've got a family emergency."

"That man—the investigator. He's working for you."

He bit back a retort. "Yes, yes he is."

"He came with all that." She waved toward the writing table. "About that boy. You've been having his mother watched, haven't you? Because you want custody?"

"You watch too much television." His voice was jocular, he made sure of that, but his pulse hammered at his temples. Somehow he had to satisfy Celeste's curiosity and keep her out of his business. "Nothing like that. Custody? Get real. What would I do with a kid? I analyze 'em, I don't live with 'em."

She smiled at that, nervously at first, then more widely and with confidence. "So why do you have to go see him?"

Blurting out his intentions about that hadn't been smart. "Just to check out that everything's okay. His situation's changed." Changed? Every shred of security had been pulled away from him and he'd been shuttled off to some relative he'd never met.

"You keep tabs on him through a private investigator. Why?"

"I don't have to go into all that with you, but it's the way it had to be." Because, when the chips were down and he'd officially turned his back on the boy, he'd been unable to put him out of his mind. Making certain Ian was safe and well cared for had felt right—essential.

"You don't have whatever rights a father's supposed to have in cases like this?"

She had to leave. She had to stop asking questions he didn't want to hear, much less think about.

Her eyes flickered away, then back again. Something had changed in the way she looked at him. Wary? Questioning? He could almost hear her wondering what else she didn't know about him, just how much he'd hidden behind a false face he'd perfected for the world.

"Look," he began, stepping cautiously, thinking his way through each word before he spoke, "this isn't something I ever expected. I thought the issue had been put to bed years ago. It all happened when I was a kid—twenty-one. It wasn't supposed to become an issue again."

"Ugliness has a way of not staying dead."

"There's nothing ugly—" He made himself take a breath. Of course she thought he was keeping a dirty little secret, a secret he was ashamed of. "I know what you're trying to say. I'm being absolutely honest with you, Celeste. We've been in business together a long time." An idea came to him. "Maybe you'd feel better if we severed that now—at least until I've straightened all this out and I can come back minus the baggage again."

"No, Byron!" She fluttered around him. "Let me pour you a drink."

"It's the middle of the morning."

"I could use a brandy even if you couldn't."

"Help yourself. I've got plans to make."

The heels of her cream leather pumps were of a gold metallic material. When she moved from the rug to the rosy-hued madrona floor, the heel tips made muffled thuds.

He wanted to take a closer look at the photos of Ian. Through the years he'd avoided having Wade take any shots. Without a visual image it was easier to remain detached.

Ian hadn't needed him before—not really. He'd made sure he was well provided for, and safe. And from Wade's regular observations and reports, the boy was happy enough.

Celeste opened a cabinet fronted with etched glass, selected a decanter and brandy bubble, and poured a healthy measure of Hennessey. She drank too much but she didn't want Byron's opinion or advice on that topic.

She wandered back, a calculated, hip-swinging wander, and arranged herself in his favorite dark green leather wingback chair. She used one heel to pull the ottoman close, and stacked her feet. Celeste's legs were her most remarkable feature, not that the rest of her wasn't remarkable.

"How old is . . . Ian?"

"Thirteen."

"You haven't exactly been an active part of his life."

He hadn't been any part of his life. "No. It never worked out that way."

"So why go rushing off now? Why not get

through this season's shooting and make leisurely plans to take some time off? It would be much simpler—"

"Simpler for whom? No, that won't be possible." The truth was that he only had Wade's word for it that Ian was happy, and now, with this move, there was no assurance that life wasn't very difficult for a thirteen-year-old uprooted from home and school during early adolescence.

Celeste swirled her brandy, sniffed, tipped up the glass until she could poke the very tip of her tongue into the liquor. She kept her eyes downcast, but the affectation was deliberately sexual. He regretted the brief, intimate interlude they'd shared. The cost had been too high, but it was over and would stay that way, no matter how hard Celeste tried to find her way back into his bed.

She rested her head back. "What's she like?"

"He . . . Oh." He spread his hand over the pocket with Lori's picture inside. "A wonderful woman. That's all I'm going to say. That, and we had a child. Then something happened, something too awful to be true—only it was true. I had to make a decision and it meant I gave up being part of my son's life. As long as everything was fine with Ian, it was fine with me. Now I'm not sure he is fine, and everything's changed."

"You're wonderful," she told him, drinking more brandy. "You'll forgive me for overreacting, I know you will. And I am coming with you. You need someone to look after your needs, too."

"No, Goddammit!" So much for being the expert on controlling temper. "No, Celeste. A man has to do some things alone. But I promise you

I'll keep you in the picture—as much in the picture as you need to be to do a good job for our interests here. And I appreciate your concern." He went to the open door and stood there, pointedly waiting.

Uncurling her legs, Celeste got up slowly. She walked toward him until she was close enough for him to see tiny beads of moisture on her brow. The lady was thoroughly unnerved.

"It's about the woman, really, isn't it? You want to see if it's still as good as you remember."

Even the thought sounded disgusting. "You . . . You wouldn't understand someone like Lori. I don't want you to mention her again. Not ever. Do we understand each other?"

Pressing her glass into his hands, she made a silent "Oh" with peach-colored lips. "Forgive me. I didn't know you were in love with a saint."

Anger confused him. "Give my apologies," he said formally. "I will contact you—but I'm not sure when. Until then, you can say what I've told you to say: I've been called away on a family emergency."

She started to say something, but he turned his back on her and went to sit at the writing table. He touched nothing until he heard her footsteps on the stairs. She moved quickly and soon the front door slammed hard enough to rattle windowpanes. Defeat wasn't a word Celeste liked to include in her vocabulary.

Byron picked up the photo and looked closely at Ian. For the first time he allowed himself to wish he could see the boy more clearly.

Ian was bent over with his face turned aside to accept licks on his neck from the big, black lab he em-

braced with both arms. A thick head of blond hair
and a grin. A tan from what Byron could make out.

He pulled out Lori's photo and set it on the
table beside Ian's.

And he brought a fist down so hard the impact
made him flinch. They should all have been playing together with the dog, laughing together. And
Byron and Lori Frazer should be holding each
other while they watched their boy romp, secure
in his parents' love—their love for him, and for
each other.

He closed his eyes and rested his forehead on his
hands. He didn't want to think, not about that hospital. He didn't want to hear its sounds and smell
its smells—or see what he had seen there.

Why couldn't he forget?

"It'll get better, Byron, son."

*He tried to evade the doctor. "I'm not your son. I'm no-
body's son, never was." He took several steps along the
hospital corridor, but his legs were too heavy.*

*"Look," Dr. Harrison said, "this is a tough one. The
toughest. My God, I want to help you. Right now you
feel—"*

Byron's teeth chattered. "You don't know how I feel."

*Rubber wheels squeaked on the green and white tiles.
The doctor caught Byron's elbow and steered him closer to
one wall. An orderly in blue scrubs pushed a gurney
past—to the closed door of the room Byron and Harrison
had just left.*

*"No!" Byron yanked his arm free. "Oh, no. Not yet,
please."*

"Byron, why don't we take a walk."

The orderly had stopped. "Are you talking to me, sir?" He looked uncertainly at Byron, then at Dr. Harrison.

"Carry on," Harrison said.

Before Byron's stinging eyes, the corridor's beige walls rippled sluggishly as if they were under water.

He looked at Harrison, and the man with the gurney. They were all under water here, and sinking deeper.

"God's not finished with me yet," he muttered.

Harrison came closer, jutting his chin and frowning, his eyes vast and popping behind thick-lensed glasses. "You need some air," he said.

"Don't tell me what I need." Byron pointed to the room into which the orderly pushed his white-draped gurney. "She needs air. My wife needs air."

"I want you to lie down," Harrison said. "I'm going to give you a shot of something to make you feel better."

"Stop telling me something can make me feel better." Byron sidestepped to the opposite wall. He held out a hand to ward the man off.

Harrison shook his head and said, "Okay, okay. Coffee, then. I'll get us both some coffee. Come with me."

"She tried to laugh," Byron said. Tears burned his throat. "She tried to laugh and she said she didn't think she'd die today because God hadn't finished with her yet."

"Lori had spirit."

"She was twenty years old." He reached behind him to feel the cool wall.

"And you're only twenty-one." Harrison folded his arms and bowed his head. "Too damn young, both of you."

"Those people don't know her," Byron said. Breath fought its way in and out of his lungs at the same time. "I don't want"—he rubbed his eyes and tried to focus— "I don't want strangers touching her."

"*Byron*—"

"*I don't want them seeing her like that. Putting their hands on her.*" He made to go back the way he'd come, but Harrison stepped into his path. "*I want to take care of her. Please. I can do it. Just tell me how and I'll do it.*"

"Hell," Harrison said, almost to himself. "She's . . . Lori's at peace now, Byron. There isn't any pain, now. Just peace."

"*She never weighed anything. I could carry her where she has to go, couldn't I?*"

"*No.*"

"*Sure I . . . could. I*—" With a clicking sound, his throat closed. "*I want to hold her—just one more time. Please.*"

The doctor's hands came down on his shoulders. "*If I could change this, I would. Damn it to hell, there are never any right words. You can't hold her now, Byron. Lori's dead. You've got to find a way to let her go.*"

"*I want to die. I want to be dead, too.*"

The banging open of the door jarred his teeth together. He saw the orderly backing from the room.

This time the white drape covered Lori on the gurney. Webbing straps had been buckled over her body.

Laughter welled in Byron's chest. "*They think*"—he pointed—"*they're afraid she might run away. And they're right! Lori can really run. Give her a blue sky and soft grass and she can run . . . and run.*"

They wheeled her past.

"*Watch her,*" Byron called. He wiped the back of a hand over his mouth. "*Watch her, you hear? She's fast.*"

A nurse came to stand in front of him. He remembered her face, but not her name. "*Will you let me take you upstairs, Mr. Frazer?*" She had a light voice. "*That's where you need to be. It'll help.*"

"No." He shook his head, and shook and shook it. *"I can't. Not now."*

"Yes, you can." Her fingers closed around his left wrist. *"I'll take you. For Lori, Mr. Frazer. You told her you'd be all right. Remember?"*

"She wasn't supposed to die." Abruptly, the tension drained away. He just wanted to lie down. *"Leave me alone."*

"I don't think that's a great idea." The nurse tucked her arm firmly beneath his. *"Upstairs we go. There's someone who needs you to hold him. It's time you were properly introduced to your son."*

Beneath his face, Byron's crossed hands were wet. Tears? How long had it been since he'd cried? Not since that afternoon in a San Francisco hospital watching his young wife's body wheeled away?

Or had he last cried some weeks later, in the dark, in the bed they'd shared?

Yes, that had been it. And he'd turned his face to the wall and prayed he would one day believe what he'd told himself in a lawyer's office, that he'd been selfless in relinquishing his tiny baby boy to a couple who would never have children of their own.

Now that grateful husband and wife were dead and once more the boy was moving on, moving on to more strangers.

But this time Byron would do what he'd promised Lori, he'd try to do whatever was right.

Perhaps then he could stop hating himself.

Chapter Two

"*There's nothing I won't do for you.*"

That had been their promise to each other. Their final vow on their wedding day. Their final words to each other before they slept each night. And on the day when Lori had died, she had whispered them to Byron. He couldn't remember if he'd repeated them back. But today he could hear her voice, the way its timbre dropped at the end of a sentence.

He hadn't thought about it for a very long time, but today he couldn't keep it from his head. On the journey he'd made since early yesterday morning, he'd felt Lori with him. Perhaps she was making sure he didn't change his mind.

The thought brought a smile, the first in days that he remembered.

He'd flown from San Francisco and over the pole to London. Following in the footsteps of Ian

Spring who had been born Ian Frazer. Boy baby Frazer. Byron had been told the adoptive parents would expect to name their new son, and he'd looked at the rumpled little face and thought *"Our son,"* and *"Matthew."* Before his birth they hadn't known if the baby was to be a boy or a girl, but if they had a son, Lori wanted to call him Matthew because, she said, it meant "gift from God."

Byron had planned to break his journey overnight in London before renting a car and driving to Cornwall. Instead he'd set off within a couple of hours of landing at Heathrow.

He'd never driven on the left before. Secondary roads had seemed like a good idea until the first time he was all but forced into a hedge by an oncoming vehicle. "There's nothing I won't do for you," he had said aloud, and pointed the Land Rover firmly southwest. "Cornwall, here we come."

Jim Wade had been very thorough. So far all the details he'd given Byron had been correct. They had led him to a rental cottage in the tiny Cornish village of Boddinick, across the River Fowey from the town of Fowey. And together with the inquiries Byron had made for himself since his arrival, they had brought him here, to his knees in a foreign church.

One word was all it would have taken. *"No."* Thirteen years ago, standing in the office of a San Francisco lawyer, he could have said no. If he had, then today he wouldn't be in an ancient English church, in an ancient Cornish fishing town, trying to make a decision that could change the rest of his life.

But thirteen years ago he'd said yes, yes he

thought it would be better to give his baby up for adoption.

He'd never lost track of the Springs and Ian. The only request he'd made of his boy's new parents was that he be the one to put him in their arms. He'd done so, looking into their happy, yet anxious faces. And he'd managed to tell them his wife would have wanted him to make sure their boy was going to good people.

The Springs were good people, straightforward, hardworking, kind people. And when he'd made himself leave them, he'd started the long, long road back to feeling alive again.

Byron after Lori.

Back to school. A life submerged in learning, learning about people and what made them the way they were. And in time the raw places within him had hurt less, then less, and finally he'd been on his way into a successful career that became so much more than he'd ever hoped for.

He'd done the right thing for the boy. If anyone should know how important it was for a child to have loving, reliable parents—people who would always be there for you—it was Byron Frazer, and he could not have given that to a baby. So he'd told himself. Then he'd managed to think less and less about the child he'd given up. Ian had a good life—Jim Wade's semiannual reports assured Byron that was so—and disrupting it once Byron was secure would have been wrong for both of them.

But Ian's life had been disrupted now. Not just once, but twice. First his adoptive father had died, then, a matter of weeks ago, Ada Spring had also died, and with that news, Byron had stopped sleeping.

The notebook in his hand was expensive. Small, bound in soft black leather and bearing a discreet gold-tooled B.S.F., it was as elegantly expensive as almost everything he owned. He didn't need the notebook. Even if he hadn't had a photographic memory, he would have remembered every word he'd written.

In that San Francisco hospital, not far from the room where . . . He didn't want to think about the room where Lori died. Then he'd been a twenty-one-year-old student making his way on scholarships and the paltry money he made as a condominium security guard. There'd been no custom-tooled leather notebooks then. Byron flipped through pages without looking at any of them, and tucked the notebook back into the breast pocket of his sportcoat.

Propping his elbows, he rested his chin on laced fingers and closed his eyes. He could still change his mind. True, he only intended to check up on Ian, but he didn't even have to do that, not if he was uncertain about the wisdom of doing so. He was a psychologist, an expert on complex family dynamics. He belonged where he could observe other people's families and give advice based on learning, not here, not . . . He was scared. Damn, it was laughable. He was a fraud, a scared fraud who advised, and chided, and lectured, and quoted.

The possibility of his own reality changing everything he'd accomplished ought to stop him cold.

There was nothing he could do about the boy

now. He'd given up that responsibility, that right. Who did he think he was, God?

A coward.

He was a hollow man with nothing to offer to flesh and blood people, not if they actually threatened to encroach on his own well-ordered existence.

In this quiet place, centuries of history settled their weighty cloak about him. He was tired. Finally, after being unable to close his eyes for almost two days, he longed to sleep, to sleep and not to dream.

A swishing sound halted his exhausted drifting. The swish of nylon colliding with nylon. A woman drew level, then passed the pew without ever glancing in Byron's direction. Evidently the kneeling position guaranteed invisibility beneath these soaring Norman arches.

"Well, there you are!"

At the sound of the woman's voice, Byron jumped. Turning in the aisle, she faced his direction, and frowned. Red brows thinly penciled into permanent surprise drew together over bright blue eyes. Hair the same unlikely color as her brows curled tightly about a plump face.

"I told you not to dawdle, my boy."

She spoke not to Byron, but to someone behind him, someone whose metal-capped heels made an echoing clatter on tesselated gray stones.

"Whatever will the vicar say? Taking half the afternoon with the flowers. Hurry up, now."

Rather than speeding up, the footsteps dragged more slowly through the nave. Byron held his breath, fighting the urge to look back. The smell of old incense and older dust stifled him. Motes of the dust swirled in swords of colored light through stained glass windows. He shouldn't have come.

"Put them over there," the woman said.

The boy drew level. Byron felt him. Then he saw him, his arms full of some sort of greenery, silently, doggedly following the woman's directions.

"Make yourself useful, there's a good boy. I know you want to make me proud of you, you just don't know how. Mrs. Harding will be along any minute. She'll expect all that to be sorted. Separate it into piles on some newspaper." She paused, a peeling metal vase in each hand. "Can you do that, Ian?"

"Yes, ma'am."

Ian. Byron's heart pounded in his ears. He had to strain to hear.

Hair the same fair color as Lori's, but thicker. This was the three-dimensional Ian, not the Ian of the distant photographs. If he chose, Byron could get up and go to him, touch him, say his name.

This was a hellish mistake. What had he been thinking of?

Ian was tall for thirteen, and thin. Would his eyes be green? What would it feel like to look into his face and have him look back?

The boy didn't know him, wouldn't know him. Byron wished that truth didn't hurt, but it did.

"Here?" Ian turned, searching for something. "On the benches?"

Byron was too far away to see his eyes.

"No!" The woman tutted and plopped her fists on ample hips. She wore a much-washed floral apron over a sensible brown tweed skirt and matching woolen sweater. "I can't imagine what Ada can have been thinking . . ." She pressed her lips together and looked heavenward. "God rest her soul. But she should have taught you something."

"Mom taught me lots, ma'am," the boy said, and even at a distance Byron saw red stain his slender face.

"I've told you to call me Aunt Muriel."

Ian shifted from foot to foot. "My mom taught me plenty . . . Aunt Muriel."

Muriel Cadwen. Muriel Cadwen, sixty-three, retired spinster librarian, sister of Ada Spring, née Cadwen. This was the woman he'd traveled from San Francisco to see. Not necessarily to speak to, but to watch. He knew she did volunteer work at the local library. The man he'd spoken to on the phone there had been quick to tell Byron that Muriel and "the boy" would be at the church this afternoon.

She sniffed and planted her brown lace-up shoes firmly apart. "Of course Ada taught you things. She was my sister, you know. But she should have made sure you knew how to behave in church. And they're pews, not benches. Separate the ferns from the teasels and the ivy and put them in piles on the floor in front of the chancel rail." She pointed to the crossing in front of the nave.

The boy looked dubiously at the bundle in his arms.

"On newspaper, mind." Muriel turned away.

Ian stared at her back a moment then started dragging newspaper over the floor with a toe.

Byron itched to get up and offer to help. He mustn't. He mustn't do anything. Not yet. Maybe never. *Go to Cornwall and take a look at the boy.* That's what he'd promised himself. Make sure he's all right. Do it for Lori because she would have wanted that. Celeste, who now knew where he was, had been charged with putting out the story that Dr. Byron Frazer, behavioral psychologist and family life guru, needed a sabbatical from his office and the TV cameras. So—if he could make peace here—he'd stick around for a few weeks, maybe get some writing done, then go home to San Francisco.

Simple. Charting logical courses for humans was his forté.

So why was his heart still thundering? And why did his throat feel as if he'd swallowed a golf ball?

More footsteps approached from behind him, these with the squish, squish of rubber soles.

Muriel, who had disappeared through a door at one side of the altar steps, popped her head out again. Hitching her apron, she bustled forward. "Afternoon, Effie. Running a bit late, I'm afraid." She raised her formidable brows and inclined her head meaningfully toward Ian. "Lot more on my hands these days. If you know what I mean."

"Yes, well, I shouldn't worry." The new arrival, a weathered, gray little woman, put a basket of roses on a pew. "You're a saint, Muriel. We all say so. I can't imagine how you're managing knowing . . . well, you'll get your reward. You know that."

In the shadow of a cold pillar, beneath an unlit candle sconce, Byron edged deeper into shadow. This wasn't going to be simple. He would have to decide. Was Ian okay or not? And if he wasn't, what could be done? What did Byron want to do?

Ian kept his head bowed. He worked a branch free, then seemed undecided where to set it.

"You'll have to be quicker than that," Muriel

said, and to Effie, "I thought I'd give him something to do. He obviously hasn't had any guidance. A month he's been here and he's still reading the first book I got him from the library. Comics, he came with. And those funny skates. Wheels all in a line."

"I wouldn't have any of that. Those comics. They give children bad ideas. Violent." Effie, inches shorter than Ian, pulled the cut greens from his arms and started to sort. "You're right to give him things to do. Keep him out of trouble. And with his history . . ." She sighed.

Muriel gave an echoing sigh and trudged into a partitioned area at the entrance to a side chapel. The faded sign on a screen read CHILDREN'S READING ROOM.

Byron seethed. He realized he'd curled his fingers until his nails cut into his palms and he made an effort to relax. The two women spoke about the boy as if he weren't present. *His history*. What would they do if Byron leaped up and said, "I know his history. There's no one who knows it as well as I do. Ian Spring doesn't remember me, but he's here because of what I did"?

Light glinted on Ian's short-cropped straight hair. TWINS emblazoned the front of a white sweatshirt, and his hands had found the pockets of well-worn jeans. The all-American kid from Minneapolis, Minnesota. And every miserable line in his handsome young face said he'd jump at the chance to be right back where he'd come from.

Effie scuttled around Ian. "Sit down somewhere," she said, impatient but not unkind. "Keep out of the way, there's a good boy."

Byron closed his eyes. He had no right to interfere. *He shouldn't have come.*

"Here you are." Muriel's voice snapped Byron's eyes open again. "The text is too young, but the pictures are beautiful. Sit over there and look at it like a good boy."

Ian stared at the book Muriel had given him. He didn't move.

"Oh, you aren't trying," Muriel said, puffing with exasperation. She snatched back the book. "Go outside. Children need plenty of fresh air. They sleep better."

His face expressionless, Ian started down the aisle.

"And don't step on any graves, mind. And don't go too far. I don't want to have to look for you."

Muriel's voice followed Ian. The heavy wooden door opened, then closed with a solid thunk.

"He still doesn't say much," Effie said. She'd finished sorting. With a practiced hand, she selected roses from her basket. "I'd have thought he'd at least try to fit in."

"I'm doing my best," Muriel said. "I talked to May. Thought with her having brought up two children of her own she'd have some ideas, but you know May." She shrugged eloquently. "She does suffer so."

"Yes, poor dear. Funny how different you three sisters are. You always busy and making the best of everything. May delicate like she is and such a homebody, and Ada!" Effie rolled her eyes upward. "God rest her soul. But Ada was the wild one. Running off and marrying that American. Then living over there. And so many years between visits. When you told me she'd been widowed, I thought she'd come home then. But no. Who'd have thought she'd pass on so young? Only fifty-two."

"Ada was independent," Muriel said, her voice oddly soft. "She was never wild, not our Ada. Pretty and independent. And we got along well. That's why the boy came to me. She'd have visited more often if it didn't cost so much."

He hardly knew that he'd risen to his feet and moved to a side aisle. Almost noiseless in his boat shoes, he left the building.

Standing by an ivy-covered wall, he took in a deep breath of fresh, early June air and blinked while his eyes adjusted to pale sunlight. Set on a hill above the port town of Fowey, the church commanded a view over crooked stone roofs and steep, narrow streets, to the harbor and the English Channel beyond. In the distance and farther inland, across the slender, sparkling inlet from the sea, lay Bodinnick. With his travel agent's help, Byron had taken a summer's lease on a cottage. He wouldn't need it more than a few weeks, but the owners didn't rent for periods shorter than two months, so Byron had paid for the whole time in advance. He'd leave when he was ready.

Now he saw Ian. Sitting on a bench, almost hidden behind the gnarled trunk of a huge chestnut tree, only his right sleeve showed . . . and moved. Byron put his hands into the pockets of his own jeans and picked a path between gravestones.

The arm moved and a steady plink, plink sounded as pebbles glanced off a gray marble statue.

Byron grinned. The least he could do was divert Ian from being a "bad boy," before Muriel caught him.

If he approached from behind, he'd startle him. Backtracking, Byron made a circle, slowing down to read markers as he went. He stopped on the other side of the statue Ian had been using for target practice and pretended to study the inscription at its base.

He looked up at Ian and smiled. "Hello."

The eyes were brown, not green. Dark brown and heavy-lashed and wary. "Hi." The blond hair dramatized those dark eyes.

No feeling Byron had experienced could have been like this. His hands were numb. Ian, the boy who had been a baby the last time they'd been together, was looking at him with no inkling that they shared a past.

Stillness shrouded Byron. It began to suffocate him. He cleared his throat and said, "Nice day."

"Yeah, I guess so." The boy was too thin, his expression too guarded with a deep weariness that had nothing to do with being tired.

"You're from the States."

Denim scraped as Ian shifted on the wooden seat. "Yeah. How d'you know?"

"Wild guess." Byron laughed. He'd never felt less confident—not for a very long time. "Minnesota?"

Ian sat forward. "How'd you know *that*?"

Byron laughed again, indicating the sweatshirt. "Twins." He noted that Ian wore new, very shiny black lace-up shoes rather than the expected sneakers. "On your shirt."

"Oh, yeah." Ian plucked at the rubberized letters. A spark of animation entered his eyes. "You're from the States, too?"

The boy must have felt the immediate kinship of shared nationality. "Yes," Byron said. "San Francisco." He took a couple more steps closer.

"Yeah? I'd like to go there sometime. If I ever get out of here."

How much did Ian know about his past? "Cornwall's nice."

Ian leaned to scrabble for another handful of pebbles. "I hate it." He resumed his attack on the statue.

Careful, Byron warned himself. "Where do you live?"

"Down there." Ian nodded toward the town. "Not far from Place. You know about that?"

Byron looked at the square towers of a huge house crammed into the middle of Fowey. "Yes. Like a castle. Pretty fantastic, huh?" He also knew Muriel Cadwen lived at 4 The Rise. In the gray hours of early morning he'd stood across the street and stared at the pretty terrace house with its profusion of flowering hanging baskets.

Another rock found its mark on a cherubic cheek. "Pretty weird, calling your house Place and nothing else. This whole town and everything is so old."

Byron searched for the next question. He should have shown surprise at Ian living in England, but the slip didn't appear to have been noticed. "So you live here now?"

"Yeah."

"And you don't like it?"

"No. I don't have much choice though, not yet."

Byron didn't have to ask what was meant by that. Already Ian was planning his escape. Feeling a rush of something close to pleasure and pride was wrong, but Byron hadn't forgotten his own drive to get away from an impossible childhood, or the fact that he'd eventually made his dreams come true.

"What's so bad about Fowey?" he asked.

Ian tossed down the rest of the rocks and turned his face up to Byron's. "Everything."

The tilt of the head, the way the faint breeze ruffled fair hair to show darker tints, the pointed chin and slender neck, lightly tanned skin—all familiar. Byron's stomach made a slow, painful revolution. "Want to talk about it?" He was a stranger. Regardless of the part he'd once played, he was a total stranger and he was dealing with this all wrong. "I'm a great listener."

"Nah."

"Okay." Why would a boy bare his soul to a man he didn't know?

"My dad died five years ago," Ian said suddenly. "In the winter. His car skidded on ice."

"That's rotten." The thudding in Byron's chest started again. "My father died when I was pretty young, too. Fifteen." Not that he'd mourned the event.

Ian crossed his ankles, seemed to notice his feet and immediately stuffed them under the bench. "My mom died, too. A couple of months ago. Cancer."

"I'm really sorry." Would the boy talk to anyone this way or had he felt some bond—other than through the country they both came from? The unreality of the moment, the situation, disoriented Byron.

"Anyway, I don't have any family in the States to take me, so I was sent here. My mom's family lives here."

"I see."

Silence fell between them. Ian's hands were long and slender, but with blunt fingertips. Again Byron's insides twisted.

"You on vacation?"

"Sort of," he said. He could see the boy from time to time. Casually. Make sure their paths crossed in an easygoing way. There'd be nothing wrong with that. "Have you been to Bodinnick?"

Ian immediately looked in the direction of the village across the river. "Over there?"

"Yes. I'm staying at Ferryneath Cottage. Near the ferry and the pub." The Old Ferry Inn, a whitewashed sixteenth-century building, stood out even at a distance. It nestled at the bottom of an almost perpendicular road lined with cottages.

"I haven't been there. If you can't drive around, you have to take the ferry."

A passenger and eight-car barge wallowed laboriously back and forth all day. "That's right. You might like it over there. Good hiking. D'you like to hike?"

Ian looked dubious. "Probably. I never did any. Anything would be better than here. I never get to do anything." He flushed crimson. "I got left to my aunt. She doesn't have any kids so I guess she isn't too sure what kids do."

Byron felt a swelling sensation. Ian was under siege, facing the biggest crisis of his life, but he could still be objective enough to try to find excuses for Muriel. "Probably. What exactly do you mean by 'got left'?"

"In my mom's will." He snorted. "Kind of like a house or something. Only Mom asked Aunt Muriel if she'd take me and she said she would."

So that's how it had worked. Jim Wade was

good, but the lawyer's secretary he'd wined and dined had only been persuaded to tell him where Ian had gone and to whom—not the legal aspects of the arrangement.

"When do you go back home?"

Byron started. There was wistfulness in Ian's brown eyes. "Not for a while. Probably not 'til September." Damn, he had to think before he spoke.

Ian turned sideways. "Yeah? That's a long vacation."

"I'll be doing some work here." If he could concentrate. Why had he said he'd stay that long? It didn't matter, they weren't going to get close enough for the boy to care.

"What kind of work do you do?" Ian asked.

"Writing. Stuff like that." He took a deep breath. "Why don't you come over and visit? I could take you for a hike on Hall Walk. That's where—"

"Yeah, I know. Aunt Muriel told me about a king who got shot over there in 1644 or something."

"Shot at," Byron corrected. "King Charles I. But it was a fisherman who died."

"She wouldn't let me visit."

"Sure she would." Now he sounded too eager. It was a wonder the boy wasn't already figuring him for a pervert. "Well, you're probably right. But if your aunt gives you some time off, ask if you can come over."

Ian got up. "I could. D'you like baseball?"

He hated it. "Love it."

"Football?"

"The season's finally getting almost long enough." And he was a liar. "More bowl games every year."

"You said it! Isn't it great? I guess you're for the 49ers?"

Byron's brain scrambled. "Er, yes." Inspiration hit. "I've always kind of liked the Vikings." This was where research paid off.

"Yeah?"

"Oh, yeah. They're cool."

"Cool! That's my team. Maybe I could ask my aunt if I could take the ferry over sometime and we could talk ball."

"Do you play sports at school?"

Ian made a wry grimace. "Nah. I was on the swim team back home is all. But I liked fooling around with my friends. We had pickup games all the time. Everyone plays soccer here. I guess that's okay, only I'm not any good at it."

"What do you like to do for a hobby?" He couldn't detain the boy much longer, yet he dreaded ending the conversation.

Ian used the toe of a shoe to make patterns in the dust. "Nothing much. I like music." He glanced up and Byron held the breath he'd taken. Naked longing shone in the boy's face. "I used to play the guitar," he said.

Byron felt the breeze, smelled freshly cut grass, and sensed the sky's blue at the edges of his vision. All he could concentrate on was the desperation in Ian Spring's brown eyes. Fate could be damn mean-spirited. Why did the kid have to be crazy about the one thing that brought Byron true peace—music, in particular the music he made himself—on the guitar? And why did he have to deal with the clear vision of Lori playing, Lori who had played better than anyone he'd ever known?

"My mom and dad paid for me to have lessons," Ian continued. "And after Dad died, my mom said he would have wanted me to go on having them, even though we didn't have a lot of money."

"So you did go on," Byron said and cleared his throat.

"Yeah."

"You must be pretty good."

Ian jerked the corners of his mouth down. "I used to be."

Seconds slid by, and Byron's too-vivid memory threatened to hurtle back to places he didn't want to go. "You mean you're a bit rusty at the moment?"

"Maybe. Aunt Muriel doesn't like any noise in the house." He shrugged. "So I don't play much."

An idea sprang instantly to life. "You could take lessons again. That would give you a chance to play."

"She said there's no one here to teach me. Then there's—" He brought his lips together and looked away. Byron saw him swallow.

"What?"

"Oh, money, I guess."

"I'll teach you." Byron's gut contracted. "I've never given lessons, but I've played for years. I picked it up myself, then finally got some instruction when I was in college." Despite the bitter-sweetness of the memories, he grinned. "Actually I got a lot of instruction in college. I met a girl who played the guitar like no one you ever heard. She wasn't so hot at math. I helped her get through her courses. She taught me to play a pretty mean guitar. Fair, huh?"

Ian wrinkled his nose. "I guess. Would you really teach me?"

The way Byron's spirits lifted was nothing but

bad news. "Sure I would." Getting involved here wasn't what he'd planned. "And we could spend some time just jamming as well. Sometimes that's the best part, huh?"

"Oh, yeah. Boy, that would be great." The longing was there again. "But it probably won't happen. She won't go for it."

Byron wanted to argue. A bad idea. "Here." He reached for his notebook, tore out a page and scribbled. "This is my name. Byron Frazer. And my telephone number. Your aunt can call me there. Or you can." He stood up and handed the sheet to Ian. "At least give it a try and ask."

"Maybe." The paper was tucked into a pocket. "I'm gonna see if it's time to go back to her house."

Not home. *Her house.*

Byron fell in beside Ian and they walked in silence toward the church. The scent of carnations and hyacinth wafted by in drifts. Overhead the occasional mound of puffy cloud broke an otherwise clear cerulean sky.

"My name's Ian. Ian Spring." He kept his eyes on the ground.

"Okay, Ian."

"Just in case I do call."

Byron could hear how badly he wanted to come, if only to talk to someone from home. "Right." *Dammit*—what if Muriel Cadwen knew his name? After the initial meeting with the Springs, the adoption had become closed, though they had met him and heard his name.

"You going into the church?"

He hadn't thought where he was going. "I left my glasses in there," he improvised. For some reason he wasn't ready to leave. The door stood open now and Byron followed Ian into the gloom. Ian immediately slipped into the nearest pew. Byron hesitated, then headed around to the side aisle again. He'd have to at least appear to be looking for the glasses that were already in his pocket.

"That about does it." The woman called Effie trotted through the door beside the sanctuary. "Very nice, too. I don't know how we'd do without the vicar's roses."

"Not nearly as well," Muriel said, appearing and shutting the door. "Oh, dear. I'd better find that boy."

Effie stopped in the act of pulling on a pink cardigan. "We worry about you," she said. "Even Reverend Alvaston seems quite in a dither about it all."

"You don't have to worry about me," Muriel said, but her voice took on a thinner note.

Byron stood still and glanced back to where Ian sat. There was no question that he'd be able to clearly hear whatever the women said.

"We do anyway," Effie continued in an enthusiastic tone. "It's one thing when you know what you've got to deal with. You don't. And that's too much. Ada should never have left you with such a burden." Her eyes turned predictably in an overhead direction. "God rest her soul."

"Yes. But I promised I would look after him if something happened." Muriel took off her apron and folded it. "I'm managing."

Effie puffed up her chest. "Of course you are. You're the kind who always does. And there aren't enough like you. But after all, who knows what kind of background a boy like that really had?"

A boy like that. Byron felt glued in place. His blood seemed to stop pumping. He dared not look at Ian again.

"I told you I'm managing," Muriel repeated. "If he was good enough for Ada, he's good enough for me."

"That's all very well," Effie said. "But the chances are there's bad stock there. For all you know his mother wasn't . . . well, you know . . . she got into trouble. That kind of thing comes out in the end."

Muriel picked up a black purse and pulled its double handles over her wrist. "You're probably right. I only hope I'll know what to do if it does."

"But should you have to?" Effie's weathered-apple face took on an even more pinched appearance.

"I have to do what my sister wanted." Muriel's chin jutted. "She adopted the boy and she loved him without knowing any more about him than I do. He wasn't wanted, that was all. We Cadwens stick together. I'll see it through—I'll keep him until he doesn't need a family anymore. I couldn't live with myself if I didn't."

Byron spun around, his throat so tight he felt sick.

The back pew was empty.

So much for worrying about Muriel recognizing the name Byron had written down for Ian. At least that was something.

Effie finished putting on her cardigan. "You Cadwens may stick together. But I hope you don't regret this. After all, *he* isn't a Cadwen. It isn't as if he's even blood."

Ignoring any effect he might have on the two

women, Byron sprinted outside and strode down-hill, looking left and right. There was no sign of Ian.

The gate to the churchyard stood open and Byron guessed the boy had left, run off, either to "her house" or to some other place where he could be alone with his thoughts.

If he hunted, he'd eventually find him.

A few yards down the hill toward Fowey, Byron stopped. He wasn't ready to talk to Ian again. Before he did, he must think very carefully about what he ought to do.

What would the boy say if Byron decided to take that step he'd never planned to take? How would a thirteen-year-old respond to being told, *"Ian, your real mother was my wife"*? Byron scrubbed at his face. How did you tell a boy, *"I'm the one who signed away his right to be your father"*?

Chapter Three

Whistling, Jade Perron sorted through a jumble of keys in a box wedged between the seats of her van. She found the one she needed and hopped out onto the cobbled yard beside Ferryneath Cottage.

"Here we are, Rose," she said to the very small five-year-old buckled into the passenger seat. "Sit tight, sweetheart, and I'll get you. Don't forget your bag."

Jade walked around and lifted Rose out. The child wrapped her arms around Jade's neck and looked into her face. "Daddy says you're our angel," she said, lisping through a space where she'd lost a baby front tooth. She gave a big smile that wrinkled her nose. "He says you won't go away from me."

Rose's daddy knew only too well that she would repeat whatever he said about Jade. Did he think she was fool enough not to know what he wanted?

Despite the affair he'd had while they were married, the one that had produced Rose, he'd begun angling to get her back. She hugged Rose tighter and inhaled the scent of baby shampoo on her hair.

"You won't go away from me, will you?" Rose said.

Jade closed her eyes and said, "No, of course I won't, sweetheart. I live in Fowey and so do you. I'm there for keeps."

"Keeps?"

"Forever." Jade almost choked on the word. She loved her hometown, but she didn't love her life there. She didn't *have* a life there and part of that was the fault of Doug Lyman, Rose's daddy and Jade's ex-husband.

No, she had to be honest or she had nothing left of who she really was—or who she'd hoped to become. In their younger school years, they'd been friends. Friendship had progressed into a teenage romance and Jade had been thrilled to be the center of handsome Doug Lyman's attention. He'd wanted to marry right out of school and Jade's parents had thought that a fine idea, but she wanted to go to a trade school, and she held fast to her plans. By the time she started work, she was ready to do what most young women in the area didn't do, work and provide for herself. Jade wanted to be independent.

"I'm glad Mrs. Tilly couldn't take me today," Rose said of the lady who ran a small day-care facility in the town. "I love it when I can come and help you."

Jade smiled at that. "I love it, too. You're a good helper."

It had taken Doug four years to beat down Jade's objections to becoming his wife, but he'd managed and she'd regretted giving in almost from the day he'd put a ring on her finger. Doug didn't want a ring himself. *Daft for men to wear rings. It embarrasses them in front of their mates.* Why hadn't she heeded all the signs that they were going to fail together?

Why hadn't they at least had a child to show for six years of marriage? Of course she loved Rose. Of course she'd never leave her as long as the child needed her around sometimes. But Jade wanted her own baby, her own toddler, her own growing child. She couldn't be sure she'd ever had a talent for making a man happy, or for being fulfilled by a man, but she did know she'd make a wonderful mother.

She wanted to be a mother.

She wanted her child to have a father.

She wanted her child to know, without question, that her parents loved each other and would never part.

She wanted to be free to grow and to be all she could be.

She didn't know how long she could go on exactly as she was but she didn't think it would be too much longer. Somehow she would find a way to look at men again—look at them as potential loves, potential lovers, as friends to be trusted, and as people who could help make a family too strong to be breached.

Almost every penny she made went into the bank. If she found someone who wanted what she wanted, and they decided to go forward together, Jade intended to bring a solid monetary contribution into the partnership. And she'd always manage to do her share so that she could insist she keep her own bank account, rather than repeating the old nightmare Doug had demanded. Everything they'd had, he put into an account in his name. Jade had suffered through the frustration of having to ask for what she needed.

She'd cuddled Rose long enough for now. "Down you go, missie. Time for me to get to work."

The child trailed a worn, plush Winnie the Pooh backpack by its straps and looked up at Jade. "Dog's coming too, isn't she?" she said.

"She's coming," Jade assured her. "Come on, Dog," she called into the van's recesses, and waited for her random-bred sidekick to scrabble her way out into the dawn of what promised to be a great day.

Rose tossed down her backpack, sat on the cobbles, and wrapped her arms round Dog's neck. If dogs could roll their eyes, Dog would be doing just that, but she sat, too, and submitted to being adored.

Pink-washed Ferryneath Cottage perched above the water like a cheerful, if peeling, old lady wearing a hat made of crooked stone slabs. A fairy tale cottage, Jade had always thought. Jade cast a critical eye over window boxes and trim badly in need of a fresh coat of white paint. Dealing with any leaks would be the first priority.

She went to the kitchen door and let herself in—and stopped on the threshold.

A man about to pour coffee into a mug also stopped.

Jade held the door handle firmly, gauging how

long it might take her to grab Rose and make it back into the van. "Who are you?" she asked.

He set down the coffeepot and strolled to the table. "Do you usually unlock other people's front doors at dawn and walk in?"

What did they call people who took over houses that didn't belong to them? Squatters? "Who are you?" she repeated.

"Who are *you*?"

The tone of his voice wasn't exactly threatening, but it was tough enough to make Jade nervous. He didn't look like someone who might wander into a vacant cottage in search of a free bed. True, his dark curly hair stood on end and heavy beard stubble covered a good deal of his face, but he was a well-built man and certainly a confident man—even if he was dressed only in white boxer shorts he'd obviously slept in.

Jade weighed her responsibility to the owners of Ferryneath Cottage against potential risk to her own safety. This man looked fit, but so was she, and she'd bet on herself to make it into the middle of Bodinnick's main street—lane—and yell for help before he caught her. And unlike in those big places in other parts of England, around here people looked after each other.

He surprised her by smiling and batting the side of his head with the heel of his right hand. "They forgot to tell you when I was arriving, right? You're the maid. I'm sorry, but I guess I'm not clicking over too swiftly yet. I'm glad to see you. This place could use a good cleaning."

She was a woman in overalls and that made her a maid? "What are you doing here?"

"I'm living here. For now."

He wasn't from around here. He was different, American perhaps. If she'd seen him before, she wouldn't forget him. Very nice looking. He was certainly comfortable wearing nothing but underwear in front of a strange female.

"Did you hear what I said, ma'am?"

"Er, no." She tore her eyes from the shorts and smiled brightly, then frowned. "I'm not the maid. What do you mean, you're living here?"

"I suppose there's been a mistake," he said, and snapped his fingers. "You've got keys. Did they rent the place to you, too?"

Jade studied his lean face checking for signs of lingering intoxication. "Are you saying you've rented Ferryneath?" His green eyes were clear. He appeared perfectly sober.

"Exactly," he said, crossing his arms over a broad chest covered with curly, dark hair. "For the summer. At least two months, anyway. They don't rent for shorter periods. I've already paid a security deposit, paid up the two months, and signed a lease."

Jade digested that before saying, "Well, we'll just have to make the best of it, I suppose. I expect you'll be out a lot anyway."

He gave a short laugh. "Something tells me we aren't communicating. This isn't a boardinghouse. It's a single-family lease property and *I'm* the current single tenant."

"Well, I suppose that's something." Jade glanced around. Pale green wallpaper dotted with assorted grinning teapots gaped at the seams. "At least I won't be wasting time falling over a bunch of people. I'm used to doing things my own way. I expect to be here about four weeks, unless something comes up to keep me longer."

"Really?" He smirked; there was no other word for it. "Perhaps we'd better stop talking in code and find out exactly what's going on here. Are you telling me you've rented this cottage for four weeks?"

Jade raised her eyebrows. "Rented? Good grief, no." She indicated her white overalls. "I'm here to redo the place—completely. A top-to-bottom, everything-inside-and-out, job. If the owners weren't so cheap, I'd have taken care of a good deal of things last year and there wouldn't be such a mess to deal with now." She shrugged. "But what can I tell you? They are cheap. This time they're so cheap they've rented the place out to you so they won't lose money while I'm working on it. It doesn't help much that the winter was so hard. The trim's going to need burning off."

He screwed up his eyes at her, half turned away, and turned back again. "Let's get this straight. You think you're going to do something or other to the paint around here?"

"Yes," she said patiently. "I'm a painter and decorator and I do a lot of work for Curtis. That's the rental agency you used, right?"

"Right." He glanced in the direction of his very long, very muscular legs and finally seemed to register that he was talking to a woman he didn't know, early in the morning, in his underwear. "Wait here. I'll be right back."

Jade couldn't recall seeing a better pair of male legs.

Two long strides took him from the room and Jade heard his feet thunder up the stairs. A glance outside showed Rose and Dog in much the place as she'd left them. Then Jade barely had time to peer into a cupboard—where a jumbled assortment of groceries confirmed the man's occupancy story—before the footsteps sounded again and he arrived back in the kitchen zipping up a pair of faded jeans. He hadn't bothered with a shirt.

"Completely redone? Is that what you said?"

"Yes. That's exactly what I said," Jade told him.

Dog, who had an uncanny habit of timing her appearances for maximum effect, chose that moment to slide into sight on her short, probably basset hound legs. She shook herself, sending water flying, and flopped down on the floor. Rose must have turned on the hose.

"From what I've seen so far this morning," Jade said to distract the man's attention from the dog, "I've got a fairly good idea what needs doing. Everything."

"But—" He came around the table until he stood, looking down upon her. "But why wasn't I told?"

It had been years since Jade had stood in a kitchen with a man, early in the morning. There was an intimacy about the moment. She'd like to enjoy it, to enjoy something she'd never had—the conviction she was with someone strong and independent, exciting perhaps, but honorable.

This was turning into an amazing morning. Now she'd started weaving dreamy scenarios around a total stranger. She'd better do something about the need that showed signs of beating its way out of her.

"I asked," Byron said, faint color rising in his

ace, "why I wasn't told you were supposed to come."

Dog shook herself again, spraying both Jade and the man. He stared at his damp jeans, then at Jade again and said, "Well?"

"I don't suppose they thought it was necessary. If they thought about it at all. My schedule's always fixed a year ahead. Never changes much."

"A year ahead?"

"Always."

"That's ridiculous."

"It works for me."

He brushed absently at his jeans. "Outside with you," he said to Dog. "Go home."

"She belongs to me," Jade said. "Her home is wherever I am."

"You bring a dog to work?" He managed to make everything about her sound outrageous.

This was wasting precious time. "Excuse me. I need to start bringing in supplies."

"Just a minute." He put himself between Jade and the door. "Let's talk about this. There's got to be something that can be done to rearrange your schedule."

Behind him, the door opened a little wider. With a squelch, squelch coming from her purple plastic sandals, Rose ventured into the kitchen, leaving soggy prints on the linoleum as she came. Jade barely stopped herself from grimacing.

"I'm Byron," the man said. "Byron Frazer. I'm from California. Tiburon. Just out of San Francisco."

"Nice to meet you. I'm Jade."

At last he heard Rose's squelching sandals and

turned around. A vast quantity of long, dark curls sprouted in all directions around Rose's small, pale face. Rose had her Winnie the Pooh backpack by the straps again and she held it before her while she frowned up at Byron Frazer.

"This is Rose," Jade said quickly. "A very good friend of mine. Come on in, sweetheart."

"Hello, Rose." Frazer turned amazed green eyes on Jade. "Does she go everywhere you go, too?"

His tone brought out her stubborn streak. "When she needs to. School's out today and the day-care place didn't have room for her." Doug Lyman had started an affair with Rose's mother some months before Jade found out. By that time the woman was pregnant. Jade detested Doug, but he tried to be a good father and she gave him credit for that.

Frazer spread his hands. "Didn't you tell me you don't like anything—anybody getting in your way?"

Jade didn't answer.

"How many more little helpers are we expecting?"

Jade ignored him again. "Let me get my equipment in, Rose, then I'll find you somewhere nice to play." She left and went to the van to start carrying in supplies.

"Look"—Frazer followed her outside—"there's been a mistake."

"I agree. Why don't you call up Rube at Curtis's and ask to be moved." The idea of an occasional glimpse of a very attractive man held some appeal, but not if he didn't want her around. "The season hasn't really started yet. There's bound to be a vacancy somewhere."

He stepped back to allow her to pass with two

buckets of paint and almost tripped over Dog, who had trotted after Jade. "Hell! I'm *not* moving. Let me carry those for you."

"Thanks, but it's not necessary," she said, but she liked the offer just the same.

"Yeah, well, they're too heavy for you."

Jade didn't tell him he was no judge of what was too heavy for a woman, even a small, rather insignificant-looking woman. What was there about a man showing basic protective instincts that made some females glow inside? Jade was glowing—just a little.

"Okay." He strode along beside her, taking one step to every two or three of hers. "This is how it is. I just got settled and nowhere else is going to have the view of the river and harbor I've got from here."

"I know." Jade carried the buckets into the kitchen. "It's my favorite. How long have you been here?"

Once more Ferryneath's annoyed tenant faced her across the table. "I arrived five days ago. Look—"

"Isn't the view of the harbor super at night? With the lights on the water?" He'd get used to the idea of her being here.

"Yes. Look—"

"I'm going to get the bedrooms done first. Then the outside. Then I'll move back inside. I've got the weather patterns around here down to a fine art. July's often rainy. I will have to check the windows for leaks sometime today." She headed back outside and dragged a dolly from the back of the van. On this she loaded her toolbox, paste, brushes, and the wallpaper Curtis had selected for one of the bedrooms. On top she balanced the collapsed table she used for sizing and pasting the paper.

When she got back into the cottage, pausing to heft the dolly over the threshold, she found the man—wearing wire-rimmed glasses—poring over a sheaf of papers on one of the counters. Rose stood beside him and he ruffled her curls absently.

"I'm calling the rental agency," he said. "They didn't mean you to come. I think there's been a mistake."

"There hasn't," Jade assured him. "Take it from me. This is the right day." And Curtis knew better than to meddle with the timetable for Fowey's busiest and most reliable painting and decorating firm.

"There *is* a mistake." He marked a spot at the top of a page and reached to haul the phone closer. "You said your name's Jade?"

"Yes, Jade." The glasses suited him.

"Who did you say you were from?"

She stopped and looked at him—more or less. "I didn't. I'm from Perron and Son."

He frowned at her. "Perron? Haven't I heard that name before?"

"If you've been here five days, you must have. It's a very common name in these parts."

Dog stretched her considerable length on the white linoleum and yawned. Rose whooped, and dashed to lie down beside the dog.

"Jade, right?" the man said, looking slightly wild-eyed. "That is what you said?"

"Mm. Several times."

He glanced at her and frowned. "You've got blue eyes—dark blue—not green."

She stared at him incredulously. "Most babies are named at birth. I was."

He said, "Yes," as if he didn't know what she was talking about.

"Newborn infants' eye color usually changes anyway."

"In other words, why would your name have anything to do with your eyes?" He jabbed at the paper. "Will I get these people at the St. Austell number?"

"Probably. Are you sleeping in the front bedroom?"

"Yes."

"I'll start in the other one."

"No!"

Jade almost dropped the hammer she was holding.

He smiled an almost sheepish smile. "Sorry. Didn't mean to shout. But this is exactly what I *don't* need right now. Would you mind if we had a little chat?"

What had they been having for the last thirty minutes? "I suppose not." Experience had taught her that the reasonable approach invariably won out over aggression. But she'd listened to an angry man's raised voice too often, and even though this was different, it frightened her. She dropped to her haunches and gathered Rose into one arm. With the other hand she stroked Dog's bristly, black and brown spotted white fur. "I am on kind of a tight schedule, I'm afraid. But I can spare a few minutes."

"You do understand that it isn't you, specifically, that I object to?"

She drew a blank in the answer department. This was already becoming a sensory overload, especially since she was out of practice interacting with a man on almost any level.

"It's just that this is a tense time for me. I came here for a few weeks of absolute peace and quiet. You can understand someone needing that, can't you?"

"Oh, yes." The fact that most people she knew rarely had the luxury of even a few days off wouldn't interest him.

"So you won't be offended if I arrange to get your schedule changed?"

Jade let Dog take the hammer between her teeth.

"Nice dog." He sounded awkward.

Let him suffer. "Thanks. I usually get comments about unfortunate canine liaisons, but I've always preferred mutts."

"What's his name?"

"Her. Dog."

He worried his lower lip. "Yes. Does she have a name?"

"Dog. That's her name."

"Ah," he nodded. "Cute. Rose is lovely, but I don't have to tell you that." He smiled at the child and Jade could tell the smile was effortless.

"Is it okay if I get started while you make your call, sir?"

"I guess so. It's Byron."

"Come along Rose." She picked up the toolbox and made a move toward the hall. The man stood between Jade and the door.

"You're sure you're going to do this?"

"I have to. Is it all right if Rose plays in the sitting room? She won't make a mess."

"It'll be a waste of time to start, then have to top again."

"That won't happen, sir." Holding Rose's hand, he took another step toward him.

He took off his glasses. His eyes slanted slightly upward. Jade liked that. There were traces of gray in his hair. The lines around his eyes were deep. He'd laughed a lot—frowned a lot?

"I'll make that call then."

"You do that. It'll make you feel better. More settled."

He turned aside, but not far enough to allow her to pass with ease. "After I get through to them, I'll come and let you know what they say."

"You do that." Standing close to him, Jade had to raise her chin to meet his eyes. Up close, she saw black and yellow flecks in the irises. His pupils dilated . . . and his lips parted. It had been a long time since she noticed a man this minutely. Maybe she never had, but this was one peculiar day.

She edged a little farther past. "The front bedroom, you said." Now she could smell him—clean, with a hint of soap and fresh linen. And she could feel his warmth.

He didn't respond.

"You said you were sleeping in the front bedroom?"

"Yes." His gaze dropped to her mouth.

A thought struck hard. "Oh, dear. Is . . . um, is someone still asleep?"

He looked blank.

Dog chose that moment to drop the hammer

and sit back to scratch a floppy ear. Jade set down the toolbox and bent over—and her face collided with a hard shoulder as the man also stooped to retrieve the hammer.

"Sorry." He caught her forearm and held on until he'd rescued the tool. "Who would still be asleep?"

His biceps were hard, his skin smooth. "Oh, I don't know, it was just a thought."

A faint smile twitched at his lips. "I'm all on my own here."

Jade felt hot, and foolish. "Ah." This was dumb. She was actually responding to a man she'd only just met—a stranger who wouldn't notice her if she weren't pushed into his space, a stranger who was doing his best to get rid of her. "I'll just go on up then."

"Mm." He still held her forearm.

"Okay." Jade drew in a deep breath and immediately wished she hadn't. His glance moved lower. She usually tried not to draw attention to her meager stature. Her insignificant face wasn't something she could disguise. "Anyway, you make your call."

She eased past, drawing her arm from his hand, and led Rose into the tiny, dim hall. When she looked back, Byron Frazer was watching her, an oddly speculative expression on his face. He bent over to pick up the toolbox she'd forgotten to retrieve, and handed it to her.

Her own vulnerability had made her careless, and stupid. She kept a firm hold on Rose's hand and, instead of putting her in the sitting room alone, led her to the stairs and started up. Dog fell in behind.

The man's presence was something she felt even before she stopped and turned. He leaned against a doorjamb—watching her again. No trace of a smile softened his face.

With a thudding heart, Jade nodded, and continued up the stairs, forcing herself not to rush. Her cell phone was in the tool box. Apparently he'd lost interest in checking up on her. Jade would get herself and Rose into as safe a place as possible, then find out just how much danger they might be in from Byron Frazer.

Chapter Four

Perplexed, Byron had watched this Jade Perron climb the stairs. A small person with masses of extraordinary long, black hair, she clutched the child's hand while the incredibly ugly dog leaped upward in hot pursuit—leaped as well as a dog could on very short legs and splayed feet.

When Jade had glanced back and seen him, she looked closed and suspicious. He really did get the feeling she expected to win the battle and send him packing. He smiled faintly. She was part of the narrow world he'd found in this insular Cornish place. All of the locals seemed to dismiss any world outside their own, and he was a "foreigner" and therefore not to be taken seriously.

The wary, blue-eyed lady had managed to make him hunt for words. Quite a feat considering she was dealing with the famed "Tell Dr. Frazer," the psychologist guaranteed to shoot from the hip, no

punches pulled, while he mesmerized millions
with his silver-tongued, but hard-line advice.

All that seemed far away and long ago—and
vaguely embarrassing when viewed from the position he was in now.

In the kitchen once more, he closed the door
and phoned the rental agency in St. Austell. Only
minutes later he hung up again. "Hell," he muttered, his teeth on edge from talking to Jade's
"Rube." "These people make laid-back sound like
hyperactive." Good old Rube had assured him
she'd do her best to find him alternate accommo-
dations, if that's what he decided he wanted, but it
might be that he'd have to pay more, and didn't
he want to think about that? In other words, he
could go if he liked (other than request a refund),
but Jade stayed put—although if he wanted to call
the outfit she worked for, well, that was his business.

The phone rang. He snatched the receiver,
preparing to tell Rube she had the order of things
all wrong.

"Is that you, Byron?"

Celeste. Damn, he'd told his secretary not to tell
anyone where he'd gone, not even his indefatigable
dynamo of an agent. Especially not her. But he
should have known Celeste Daily would browbeat
poor Angela until she caved in.

"Byron? Answer me."

"Yes, Celeste." Carrying the phone, he dropped
into a chair. "I'm not in the mood to talk to you. I
left a message to say I'd contact you when I was
ready."

"What way is that to treat me, darling?" She was
shrieking now. Byron hated it when Celeste—or

anyone else—shrieked. "I'm your *agent,* for God's sake. Your *best* friend. Is this any way to treat a best friend? Sneaking off in the night like a thief and leaving me to spend an entire *week* searching for you. I've been *beside* myself, I tell you. *Beside* myself!"

Beside herself worrying that she might be losing money on the appearances he'd canceled. As his finances went, so went Celeste's. She'd virtually made his career her life's work. "I thought I'd made it clear that this was something I had to do. If I didn't, I will now. I have to do this, Celeste. This isn't a good time for us to talk. Why don't I get in touch with you later?" Much later.

"No, Byron. Absolutely not. Don't you dare try to close me out of whatever's going on. When you said you had to leave California, you didn't say you were heading for some godforsaken little hole in *Cornwall, England.* I've got to look after you. You're either in some sort of personal trouble you're afraid of, or you're having a breakdown. This is a crisis. I'm already in Seattle. I'm catching the next flight over the pole. I'll be in Heathrow by mid-afternoon tomorrow. I'll give you the flight number. Meet me, darling. Promise you will. We'll spend a few days in London and have a wonderful time together. We don't even have to talk business for a day or two if you don't want to. Then I'll take you—"

"I won't meet you. Don't come."

The only sound for seconds was the faint crackle of the overseas line.

"You missed the lecture in Chicago," Celeste said finally.

"I gave them a week's notice. And I told you to

put everything on hold until I made contact with you."

"A *week?* A *week,* you say. As if you didn't know how far ahead these things are scheduled. This is too much, Byron, really too much."

"Have you informed everyone else who needs warning that I can't appear in the near future?"

"You can't do this," Celeste shouted. "You can't just drop out of sight without an explanation."

"I have no problem with you putting out a press release stating that a personal crisis has intervened."

"They'd *crucify* us. Oh, my God. Think how people would speculate. What's the matter with you? You have to be squeaky clean, you know that. They'll come up with a million sleazy rumors."

He didn't answer.

"I'm coming, I tell you. This isn't like you and I want to know what's going on. You can't rush halfway around the world without telling me first."

"The hell I can't, I—" A slight sound made him look around. Jade was trying to tiptoe past. She held Rose's hand again, and the dog trotted at her side. He met those blue eyes again. She raised delicate brows and pointed first at her dolly, then hooked a thumb toward the door to the rest of the house. Byron shook his head emphatically. He covered the receiver and said, "Please wait here. This won't take long."

"Byron, darling. *Please.*"

"Don't push, Celeste."

"Don't *push?*" She expelled a hard breath. "You have a public. You have responsibilities to that public, and to your practice."

"I'm way ahead on my taping schedule. My prac-

tice is my concern, not yours. My patients have
been given the option to see a colleague or, if they
feel able, to wait for my return. I'll also deal with
emergencies by phone."

He found, even as he spoke to Celeste, that he
couldn't take his eyes off Jade Perron. She had
dropped to sit cross-legged on the floor beside the
dog. Her springy black curls arched away from a
point in the center of a high forehead. She had a
perfect, heart-shaped face. He'd never seen anything quite so intriguing—other than in paintings
of Victorian girls who hadn't yet put their hair up.
She was very pale-skinned, and men who went for
flamboyant beauty would find her too subtle. He
could hear her whispering softly to the mutt while
she kept an arm around Rose.

"I'm coming," Celeste said, controlling her
voice this time. "And I'm going to bring you back
with me. That's that."

"No, it's not." He should have put his foot down
with overbearing Celeste years ago. "As I've already
explained—several times—there's something I have
to do here and that isn't negotiable."

"*There?*" The rattle of papers sounded.
"Bodinnick-by-Fowey, Cornwall. Not even a published population count on the Net, for God's
sake."

So, she'd already done her research. How like
Celeste. She'd go into shock if she had any idea
what had been running through his mind in the
past two days, even if he was totally unsure what he
intended to do about it. He was in a strange place
and in a strange mood. He was completely unset-
tled. When he thought deeply about the steps he'd
taken, he scared even himself, but he wasn't pre-

pared to leave without completing what he promised himself he'd do. Ian grew in importance to him with every hour. He had to make sure the boy would survive here and come through without being crippled by an environment that seemed impossible.

"What could you possibly have to do in a place like that?" Celeste said. "How did you find it?"

"I found it. You wouldn't be interested how. And Bodinnick may be small, but linked to Fowey, it isn't *that* small."

"Try me. Interest me."

Mollify, his defense mechanism advised. "Celeste, we've been together a long time."

"I thought for a moment you might have forgotten that."

To hell with mollifying the barracuda. Her bossiness had long ago failed to divert him. "But maybe we've been working together too long. Maybe it's time for you to use your talents on someone up-and-coming who'll be more of a challenge," he paused for an instant, then added, "and willing to be controlled."

"My God! How can you be so damnably ungrateful? How can you even suggest this? Are you trying to fire me, because if you are, you'll have a war on your hands. I'll fight you to the wall, baby. And I may be a lady, but I can fight dirty when I have to."

He swallowed the temptation to give Celeste his description of a lady, but he said, "I'll just bet you would fight dirty. Back off, Celeste."

"That private detective is mixed up in all this. Since he's the one who sent you on this wild trip, he can do the rest of whatever needs doing. Tell him to get there and deal with things. You're too expensive to be wasting time like this."

She just didn't know how to give up. "No one but me can do what has to be done. End of topic. Now back off."

"I will not let you push me aside."

Jade Perron's pale face had lifted again. She regarded him with interest. Her full mouth held a permanent, quite sexy pout. If he didn't have a clear impression that she wouldn't know how to be other than her natural self, he'd say the pout had to be practiced. In Jade's case the mouth undoubtedly came that way. She was really quite beautiful, an ethereal, somewhat undersized vision even in the unflattering overalls.

"Byron? Did you hear what I said?" Celeste said loudly. "I won't be pushed aside because you've found someone more interesting—so you think. Take it from me, it won't be a good idea for you to cross me in public." She softened her voice. "I'd have thought you'd remember how far we go back, what we've meant to each other."

"How could I forget?" Cooling things down would be for the best, at least until he got himself sorted out. "Now I'm asking you to trust me. And to cover for me . . . darling." He detested theatrical largess. "This is something I really need. This time away in total isolation. Will you trust me? If I promise to call you in a few days, say in a week? Next Monday? Please, Celeste?"

"Well." Her tone was still wounded, but more gentle, and he almost felt ashamed of his own manipulation—almost. "Byron, darling. You aren't sick, are you?"

"I've never felt better." A lie, but the reason for

his feeling rotten had nothing to do with his physical condition. "I would tell you if I was ill," he added, anticipating her next question.

By the time he finally hung up, Celeste had promised to return to San Francisco to await his call next week. She'd deal with any inquiries that came in about appearances, putting people off where necessary. Byron knew he'd need a very convincing story to appease her on Monday.

He smiled at Jade. "My agent," he said, suddenly awkward that she'd had to listen to the conversation. "Sometimes agents and their clients have different views on what's important."

"Oh."

"She doesn't think I deserve a vacation." He laughed, coughed. "Not that this is a vacation. Not really."

She bounced to her feet and looked at her watch. "May I get started now?"

"Um. I called the rental people. They offered to move me." At least she didn't give a triumphant grin. "They did say I could call your company to make sure your calendar isn't mixed up. They didn't seem to want to take the time to look up the number for me. I'm sure if I talk to your people, they'll confirm there's a mixup."

"Could be." Her smile took him totally by surprise. It intensified the tilt of her eyes and drove dimples into her cheeks. "These big outfits tend not to keep very good tabs on all the little people on their staffs. This is the number." She fished a card from behind a row of pens pocketed in her overalls bib. "There's an answering machine. Leave a message. I really must get on."

Glancing at the card he said, "Perron and Son. You said that. Same name as yours."

"Uh-huh. Perron in Cornwall is like Smith in some places."

He pulled his bottom lip between his teeth. He had the impression the lady might be enjoying some private joke.

She left with Rose perched on the loaded dolly with the equipment. He could have sworn Dog shot him a grin as she pranced behind. The situation here was getting to him. He had to keep a tight hold on himself.

Byron remained at the table and drummed his fingers on a yellow pad he'd been using to make notes for the book he already had a contract to write. Who was he fooling? How could he write anything on the inner self that might make sense when his own inner self was in turmoil?

Since Saturday he'd found three reasons to take the orange ferry boat across the smooth, silver water between Bodinnick and Fowey. He'd trailed the quaint streets, some so narrow that pedestrians had to stand on doorsteps to allow cars to pass, searching for a glimpse of Ian. 4 The Rise was a skinny terraced cottage with faintly bulging leaded windows and a riot of flowers blooming in boxes and hanging baskets. Ian hadn't come or gone from the shiny black door. But Byron discovered that the children still had a number of weeks in school before summer vacation. And they didn't get out as early each day here as they did in the States. Twice he'd strolled past the school just as students streamed out on their way home and had "accidentally" run into Ian. They'd walked a block or two together, chatting, mostly about the States, before Byron made himself turn away.

He got up and went from the kitchen into the sitting room and his own leaded-paned windows. Bodinnick eyed Fowey across the estuary, so close the ferry took only minutes to make the trip.

What should he do about Ian?

The instant a move was made to interfere with the boy's current home situation, Ian's life would be forever changed and Byron couldn't know if that was right. He couldn't know if it would be the right step for himself. His own life would also be turned upside down—particularly if he decided to do what might be necessary, and get into a legal wrangle for custody.

Overhead something scraped. And Byron winced. The scraping came again, making the light that hung from a wire in the middle of the room swing.

She was such an insubstantial creature. The idea of women doing what used to be considered purely men's jobs—and heavy work—didn't surprise him . . . except when he was confronted by someone who probably didn't reach his shoulder, someone with a face that belonged in commercials for natural soaps.

Stretching out on a puffy, rose-colored velvet sofa, he hauled an ancient black phone onto his chest and dialed the number on the card she'd given him.

"Perron and Son. This is Jade Perron. I'm sorry to miss your call. Please leave a message. I'll get back to you as soon as possible. Thank you."

So, the lady was the boss—or closely related to the boss. Which was undoubtedly why she'd insisted she knew the timetable for repairs around here was correct.

He left a message and set the receiver down gently. Sure she'd had her little piece of fun with him and he should be irritated, but he was unable to repress a smile. No wonder she'd looked so amused. He'd treated her as his inferior, and now he thought about it, that made him ashamed. He's committed the sin of putting someone in the box he'd automatically judged appropriate, and done so with very little information to go on.

Jade Perron had a very nice, husky voice, very nice indeed. Particularly on the phone. He could almost imagine her saying: "Gotcha!"

Chapter Five

"Must be nice to be able to flit around the world taking summer-long holidays," Jade mumbled to Rose. "Not for the likes of you and me, girl. Poor working types, we are." She wasn't about to remark to the child that Byron Frazer's life sounded too complicated for the simple likes of them.

At least her telephone call to Rube, she-who-knew-everything, put Jade's mind at ease about Frazer's character. He did come from a place called Tiburon, in California and close to San Francisco. He was a doctor of some kind and he wrote books. Rube thought it funny that Jade wondered if she should be afraid of him. "Clobber him with your hammer if he makes any moves on you. I never met a man who would be a match for you if you got your knickers in a twist."

Sitting on the kitchen floor and listening to him argue with his agent had revealed a few other details to Jade. He was the kind of doctor who saw patients, and gave lectures to people. An important man from the way it sounded. In other words, she wasn't in personal jeopardy.

Jade wedged herself between the wall and the head of the bed. "Too bad I don't have a little more weight to put into this." With her back against the headboard, she walked her feet up the wall, knees almost touching her chest, and pushed. The bed was old and made of very heavy mahogany. A couple more inches of progress was all she made.

"Waste of time." After a moment's rest, she crab-walked up the ghastly cabbage-rose wallpaper again, took a huge breath, let it out, and heaved.

Rose stood beside her, spread her little hands on the headboard, and pushed. She held her breath until her face turned red and Jade had to fight down laughter.

"Can I do something to help?"

Propped more or less horizontal, two feet from the floor, Jade went rigid.

"You'll hurt yourself doing that. Why didn't you call me?"

Frazer walked into her line of vision, carrying the rest of the rolls of paper she'd left on the dolly at the foot of the stairs. Dog moved close to Jade and growled, a faint rumble that meant little but usually had the desired effect. Dog wasn't fond of men, especially men she sensed were troublesome to Jade.

If the man noticed the noise at all, he showed no sign. "Please. If you'd let me help you up, I'm sure I could . . . we could do this together in a minute. The bed's catching up on the rug."

She felt a complete fool. Relaxing her leg muscles, she attempted to stand up. Instead she slammed—bottom first—to the floor, jarring her neck. "Ouch! Damn it all, anyway. Damn—" Oh, great. "Complete fool" didn't cover this. She was swearing in front of Rose, whom she tried to cushion from anything unpleasant, Rose whose eyes were huge and worried. Jade kissed a finger and tapped the little one's nose, and watched her relax almost instantly.

"I know how you feel." Frazer's voice really was nice. Soft but deep and very, very clear. He offered her a hand. "Up you get."

Unable to do otherwise unless she wanted to appear any more foolish, she put her hand in his and let him haul her to her feet. "Thanks."

"You're welcome."

She hadn't met many Americans, but those she had met all said that. *You're welcome*, and *Have a nice day*. Like some button had been pushed.

"I called your office."

She blushed, something she didn't do often these days. "Yes." That had been childish on her part. She ought to be ashamed. She was. "Sorry about that."

"Why be sorry? I left a message."

"Good." This was turning into the most frustrating morning in recent memory. She loathed getting off schedule, although he was certainly something worth spending time looking at . . . if she were still into looking at knock-em-dead men. But she'd given up the habit.

No, she hadn't. No, not one bit of it, not anymore. She wasn't about to start looking for handsome men, but she was going to allow herself to think about an occasional date with someone who didn't make her feel threatened—maybe. That would be a start.

She was going to do something about changing her life, not that Byron Frazer—Dr. Byron Frazer— entered into the picture other than playing a small part in forcing her to start examining what she'd allowed herself to become: a boring, unfulfilled woman who was going nowhere, was unhappy, and who—as of today—had decided to stop wasting time.

Jade realized she was staring at him, and he was waiting patiently for her to say something. "I'd appreciate your help with this bed. Mahogany is very heavy."

"Would you like to know what I said in my message?"

Jade pretended to turn her attention to the bed. "I should have told you who you'd be leaving your message for. Forgive me, please. Mornings aren't my best time." Now she was spilling her uninteresting personal hangups. "They bring out my evil side."

"Mine too—sometimes. Let's get this bed moved. Then I'll tell you what I said."

Did he think that by being so darned nice he could divert her?

Well, he could divert her. Very easily. She took a shaky breath and recognized the almost forgotten sensation of being vulnerable, of wishing she was more attractive, and in this case that this man were interested in her other than as a problem to be eliminated.

She'd made rapid progress in changing her attitude toward men . . .

The sleeves of the blue denim shirt he'd put on were rolled up over muscular forearms. He smoothed Rose's cheek, earning himself the fluttering, plainly trustful touch of her fingers on the back of his hand. He smiled, and Rose smiled. Then he pushed the wretched bed into the middle of the room as if it were a piece of doll furniture.

Rose said, "He's strong like my daddy," with evident awe.

"Thank you," said Jade.

"You're welcome."

You're welcome. Oh, he could definitely divert her any old time. Yet again she caught speculation in his dark green eyes.

He smiled, crossed his arms, and stood with his bare feet planted apart. "What exactly are you supposed to do in here?"

"Everything," she told him. He had the kind of legs that must have inspired whoever had invented jeans: having seen him without the jeans, she should know. "The designer paper goes. And the brown paint around the windows."

"Sound like good moves to me." He screwed up his eyes and surveyed the room critically. "Pretty dreadful the way it is."

"They want me to use acoustical tile on the ceiling. I don't like the way the stuff looks. I don't like it anywhere, but in a lovely old place like this it would be a sin. I'd rather sand the beams and oil them, then texture the plaster between."

"You've got great instincts. If you want me to put in a word for your idea, I will."

He was trying to win her over. But for what? Jade glanced at his wide mouth and decided his ploy was working . . . and she was nuts. Byron Frazer had no reason to care about her in any way. "It was very nice of you to help with the bed."

"You're welcome."

She bit the inside of her mouth to stop a laugh. He stared at her and smiled once more. Such a nice smile. Such a nice face. Better than nice.

"What else can I do to help?"

"Nothing, thanks."

When he smiled, the laugh lines at the corners of his eyes deepened, so did grooves beside his mouth. His tan suggested that, unlike Jade, he didn't spend most of his life indoors or hidden under the type of hat she used for outside work.

"Would you like me to tell you what I said on your answering machine?"

"If you like." He certainly was a big man. She liked big men. Her father was big, if stooped now, and her brother, Peter . . . and Doug.

"Do you live in Fowey?"

She hesitated. "Yes."

"Have you lived there a long time?"

"All my life."

"Is Perron your husband?"

"No. My father." She'd thought he was the one who was about to tell *her* something.

"Did you grow up helping him?"

A true third-degree. "No. I didn't come into the business until after I'd been to trade school. Then I apprenticed to my father." Would he have any idea what she was talking about?

For the first time he seemed stalled for a question. "Do you like it in Cornwall?"

"I don't think I'd live anywhere else." She'd change a lot of things in her life, erase some of the mistakes she'd made, but Cornwall was in her blood.

True she thought she'd decided to broaden her horizons—move to another town, maybe—but that town didn't have to be in another county. And she had to be where she could see Rose easily, at least until she was old enough to understand that someone moving away didn't mean they didn't care about you anymore.

"Um, do you live with your, er, parents?"

"No." She'd swear he was interested in her. That was nutty. Why would a man like him, obviously successful and wealthy, pay any attention to a simple Cornish tradeswoman? "I live in a flat over a secondhand shop," she said impulsively, unsure why she suddenly felt like volunteering personal information.

"Sounds interesting. Is it a big place?"

Jade frowned. "It's very small. Dog and I don't need a lot of room. But it's comfortable, and I love it there."

He puffed out through pursed lips, and ran a hand over his hair. "I see. You'll have made it a special place."

"Thanks."

"You're welcome."

She shook her head. "I'll go and get the rest of my things."

"What about my message?"

"What about it?"

"You don't know very much about me. Don't you think you should if we're going to be sharing a cottage?"

Sharing a cottage? "I know you're a busy man with the kind of career that means you have to have someone help you run it." And she wished she were more sophisticated so she wouldn't feel intimidated by him in some areas. "I don't think I need to know much more."

She'd pinned his age at thirty-something, his height at six-something, and the rest of him at definitely more than worth looking at. And she'd like to know him. She blushed at the thought.

He had a way of tilting his head and looking her directly in the eye, so directly she had to look away. If he noticed her discomfort, he was polite enough not to react.

"I told the machine I'm planning to spend the summer here. I'm going to be catching up on some work I've put off for too long because . . . I need to recharge a bit."

Was he someone famous enough to be known even in England? He could be. She didn't have much opportunity to keep up on celebrities, which would excuse her for never having seen him.

"I said I've been hoping for some peace. Quiet. You know?"

As in no banging and all the other things that went with her occupation. "I'll do my best to keep the noise to a minimum. This job really has been scheduled for a long time and it can't be changed now—not without disrupting my business, and forcing me to reschedule work for other people. I could lose that work if I make them upset. The work and the money. I've also got men who work for me and they don't expect sudden changes. It's not fair to them." She did sound reasonable, didn't she?

"I'm sure you will try to be helpful. And I'll try to adjust, but if it gets too much, I'll have to talk to the leasing agency again."

She raised her brows. "That's your prerogative."

"I also asked a question on the answering machine."

Jade wiped her hands on her overalls. She was unaccountably hot. "I'll be sure and listen when I get back to the office."

"Oh, I might as well repeat it in person. I rarely do impulsive things, but I'm new around here and could use some help."

"Help?"

"Yes. I want to learn as much as I can about the area. On the machine I asked if Jade Perron would consider having a drink with me on Friday evening. A drink and conversation. No strings attached."

Chapter Six

There were times when Shirley Hill's prying went too far. "I don't know anything about Byron Frazer," Jade told her, making a valiant effort to edge away from her landlady.

"Oh, you must know *something*," Shirley said. Thick, tow-colored braids slithered back and forth with the knowing waggle of her head. "You've been working in the *same* house with him for days."

"*Two* days," Jade said impatiently. "And working in the same house, but not *with* him." She liked Shirley, but frequently wished it wasn't necessary to pass through the cluttered showroom of "New to You" on the way to the flat.

"Sam says he's *really* famous. Someone on one of the yachts in the harbor—some American—saw this Byron Frazer and recognized him. He's on the telly, Jade. He's *really* big in the States."

Jade sighed. Shirley and Sam Hill were an unlikely couple. Thin, devoid of makeup, and a militant vegetarian, in her long floral skirts and shapeless gauze shirts, Shirley resembled an aging flower child. Sam Hill was a ruddy-faced ex-heavyweight boxer who was said to consume his body weight in beer in an average month. He swore good-naturedly, argued incessantly—if good-naturedly— and ran a water taxi between Fowey and the many yachts that anchored in the harbor.

"Does he hold wild parties over there?"

Jade sighed and crossed her arms. Shirley wouldn't give up without a fight for what she wanted. Jade was so tired, and so muddled up in the confusion that reigned in her head. She said, "Dr. Frazer is a very quiet and private man. He's here to work." She searched for a way to end speculation. "He's writing a book."

"A book?" Shirley's brown eyes became round. "He's a . . . He's a behavioral psychologist. That's it. I bet he's writing a book on sex!"

Jade barely contained the urge to tell Shirley she was an irritating gossip. "All the things I've seen around the cottage are about families and children. Now, I've got to get upstairs."

"Does he talk to you?"

"He's—" She should have refused to have a drink with him on Friday. The invitation must have been issued on an impulse because he didn't know anyone locally yet. He'd said as much. "We have talked a few times. He's very nice." Her acceptance had also been impulsive, but she wanted to go. She wanted to go because it would be an opportunity to be with a really interesting man of a type she'd never expected to meet, much less receive any attention from.

Jade shivered although she wasn't cold. Today

he'd greeted her pleasantly, but as if he had a lot on his mind. Then he'd gone out, and still been out when she knocked off for the day.

And she'd watched for him.

She felt desperate to get away from Shirley. "I'd better get upstairs. Dog's hungry." She had watched for Byron, looked from the windows at the slightest noise, and left the cottage feeling deeply disappointed. Like a plain teenage girl mooning over the most popular boy in the school. She disgusted herself.

"Is he good-looking?" Shirley asked, watching her too closely.

Only the best-looking man she'd ever seen. "I suppose some people would think so." He was probably regretting having asked her out. She should make an excuse and renege.

Shirley started to hum, a sign her attention had wandered as it so frequently did. She turned sideways to squeeze between tables crowded with merchandise of every description—from plastic jewelry to antique tea sets—and went behind the counter.

"Night then, Shirley."

"You're wasting yourself," Shirley said. "You know that, don't you?"

Jade bowed her head. "I'm very tired, Shirley."

"You need a man in your life—and that doesn't mean you ought to let that Doug Lyman wheedle his way in with you again."

"That will never happen," Jade said quietly. She picked up an almost new Paddington Bear wearing yellow welly boots. "I've been looking for one of these for Rose. I'll buy him."

"It's working," Shirley said, her tone grim. She reached Jade and took the bear. With her mouth

pursed and her elbows sawing the air, she wrapped
Paddington in several sheets of much-used tissue
and fastened the paper shut with a row of star and
moon stickers. "He's using that girl to get to you.
What kind of man calls his ex-wife to fill in as a
baby-sitter. Especially when his child is his by the
woman he played around with when he was married? You answer me that, Jade. You're lonely.
That's what it's all about. I'm going to find a way to
get you out of that."

"Please don't say any more," Jade said, horrified
to discover she was trembling. "I'm smarter than
you think. I know what Doug's trying to do and it
won't work. But I do love Rose and I'll be there for
her when I can."

Shirley handed over the package. "A pound,"
she said.

"Oh, it's got to be more than that. It's almost
new."

"I said it's a pound." Shirley sounded angry
enough to shock Jade. "I love Rose, too. The difference between you and me is I love Rose but it's
because she's a lovely little girl. And although we
were never blessed with children, I don't start
imagining some nice kid who comes my way is
really my kid."

Jade located a pound in her pocket and handed
it to Shirley. "Thank you," she said. "I don't pretend Rose is mine. That's what you're suggesting
and it's not true. I need to get upstairs."

Shirley turned abruptly away and skirted loaded
tables to get to the counter, where she began moving piles of books for no evident reason, banging
them down and raising clouds of dust.

With escape in sight, Jade made for the door

leading from the shop to a store room and the steps to her flat.

Dog overtook her on the dim landing and raced to wait at the slightly crooked door to what had been Jade's home for five years. "That's the girl," she said, bending to rub a short, bristly muzzle. "Guard the castle." Every day brought the same ritual and Jade took pleasure in coming home to a place where she could do as she chose without deferring to anyone else. Life might not be great, but it had been worse.

She unlocked the door and walked into the four-room flat her mother never missed an opportunity to refer to as "that chicken coop." The living room, bedroom, bathroom, and kitchen were indeed tiny, but they fitted Jade like a glove of her own making. Brilliant yellows made the small areas bright. Puffy cushions the color of sunflowers and striped or polka-dotted with red heaped a rattan couch and chairs. Polished yellow cotton drapes were drawn back from a bay window over Lostwithiel Street and early evening light cast warm shafts over the pots of fresh flowers provided from Art Perron's garden. For Jade's supposedly retired father, gaining a reputation as Fowey's premier gardener had become an obsession.

She tossed her keys onto the yellow lacquered chest that served as a coffee table and bent to unlace a tennis shoe.

"Jade!" Shirley's high voice accompanied thumping footsteps on the stairs. "Jade! Are you there?"

"No," she muttered. "That was a ghost you just told off."

"Really," Shirley said breathlessly as she entered the room, a bulging paper bag in each arm. "If my head wasn't screwed on, I'd lose it. Sam says I've got nothing between the ears but alfalfa sprouts."

Secretly, Jade thought Shirley's husband might have made a valid discovery.

Shirley cleared her throat and said, "You won't hold it against me, will you? What I said? I care about what happens to you is all. But it is past time you found yourself another man, you know."

In the act of pulling off a shoe, Jade paused, wobbling on one foot. "Don't start on that again, please."

"You can't go on punishing every male member of the species just because of Doug Lyman."

Jade almost overbalanced. "My ex-husband's history as far as I'm concerned. I don't even want to hear his name."

"Does this Dr. Frazer turn you on?"

"Shirley!"

"No, don't get mad at me. I mean it. Does he? Turn you on, I mean?"

"Shirley!"

"Oh, don't give me that shocked rubbish. I'm just being sensible. You know what they say, it's as easy to get turned on by someone rich as someone poor. And Sam says Dr. Frazer's *really*—"

"Rich? And he's really famous and who knows what else he *really* is? I can't believe you're talking like this about someone you don't even know."

"He's here, isn't he?"

"Yes, but—"

"And he's on his own, isn't he?"

"Yes, but—"

"And you're on your own—more or less—aren't you?"

"Except for enough family and friends to choke a horse."

Despite the bags, Shirley managed to shrug her bony shoulders. "There you are, then. He's alone and you're alone. I knew I saw something in your stars. I told you as much last week."

Jade sat on the couch, rested the back of her head against a cushion, and closed her eyes. "I told *you* last week that it's dangerous to live your life around all that mumbo jumbo." Even the most casual bargain hunter entering Shirley's shop was bound to be asked for an astrological sign.

"I'll let that pass."

Through slitted eyelids, Jade saw Shirley perch on a chair.

"What's his sign?"

Jade groaned.

"Never mind. I'll find out for myself. He isn't a Scorpio, is he?"

"How would I know? And why would I care?"

"Darkly sexual, they are. Still types with hidden appetites. Lustful and hot-blooded but with a cool outside that covers it all up for the innocents that walk into their hands all unknowing."

Jade opened her eyes.

Shirley squinted in deep concentration and pursed her lips again. "One minute you'll be thinking of soft music and flowers and gentle romance, the next you'll be swept into a vortex of wild passion."

"Vortex of wild passion?"

"Yes. You'll become his sex slave and be completely changed. Black satin and red silk ropes and feathers and melted margarine."

Jade sat forward. "Melted margarine?"

"Yes. You know. All that food stuff's very big now. Massage it all over, they do. To make their skin slip together, I suppose." She shivered. "Imagine that. Being massaged with melted margarine by a sexy behavioral psychologist. Ooh."

"Shirley," Jade said softly. "Why on earth would anyone use margarine?"

"Aha. You do know what I'm talking about. Nobody uses butter anymore. Animal fat's not good for you—clogs the arteries."

Jade laughed. She slipped sideways on the couch and propped her head on one hand. "Yes, indeed. Well, I'm not expecting to become Dr. Frazer's sex slave." Did she regret that? She grinned afresh. Thank God she still had a sense of humor. "I really should think about making something to eat. So, if you've got whatever you were thinking about off your mind . . ."

"I don't like that phony cream stuff you can buy."

"Neither do I . . . Phony cream?"

"Well, they do say that's something these sex addicts use for—"

"Okay, Shirley." Jade got up. "Bless you for worrying about me, but there's no need. I can assure you that if Dr. Frazer's looking for romantic involvement, he'll have his pick of the litter around here—or anywhere else. He won't look in my direction."

"You're beautiful, Jade." Shirley sounded like a defensive parent. "If he hasn't noticed, I'll find a way to make sure he does."

Jade threw up her hands. "I will take care of my own love life. Thank you, Shirley. Give my best to Sam."

"Yes, well, I will." Shirley struggled to her feet and walked onto the landing. "Oh, my. Will you look at what I'm doing. I'd forget my head if it wasn't screwed on."

Praying for patience, Jade watched Shirley maneuver a turn in the narrow space outside the door and cart the bags back into the living room.

"I don't mind saying how surprised I was."

Jade stepped back, trod on Dog, and almost slid to the floor. "What is it, Shirley? Quickly, before you forget again."

"My, touchy tonight, aren't we?" The two bags were dumped on the yellow chest. "These are for you to give to your mum."

"My mother?" Jade narrowed her eyes. "I don't understand."

"She was in earlier and picked out these things. Then she was too tired to take them with her."

Her mother had always been too tired to do most things, Jade thought, and immediately banished the thought as disrespectful. "My mother came here and bought things?" Art Perron's wife, as her mother always referred to herself, didn't "hold" with the "secondhand junk" Shirley sold, any more than she "held" with Jade living in the flat over the shop rather than at home.

"Not for herself." Shirley smiled. She might affect vagueness, but she'd already let Jade know that her mother's attitude showed. "They're for the boy."

Jade shook her head slowly.

"Ian," Shirley said, sounding irritable. "You know. Ian Spring."

"Why is she buying clothes for him?" Particularly the kind of old and out-of-date things stocked at New to You.

"Because her sister nagged . . . He needs some more things. Evidently your Aunt Muriel asked your mum to see what she could find."

Shirley wandered out again. When she turned back to pull the door shut, she said, "Find out if he's a Scorpio."

Chapter Seven

Ian Spring sat in the recesses of an overstuffed chair upholstered in dusky pink brocade. His hands were spread on his thighs and he kept his eyes lowered.

"Hello, Ian," Jade said, closing the door from the hall to the sitting room in her parents' house. "I'm glad to see you." In fact, she wasn't. She had things to discuss with her mother and he couldn't be present.

"Hi," Ian said, his voice so low Jade hardly heard what he said. He puffed up his cheeks and stared at the ceiling.

Jade glanced at her mother, who hadn't noticed her daughter's arrival. Ian needed a champion. Aunt Muriel meant well, but she didn't know what to do with a young teenage boy and he was suffering as a result. Jade felt his eyes on her and looked in his direction. Instantly he looked away.

The theme music from *Coronation Street* faded.

Dressed in a mauve chenille bathrobe and matching backless slippers, May Perron sighed, as she always sighed when her favorite television program was over, and raised her evening glass of Guinness to pale lips. A film of Ponds cold cream shone on her unlined face. Unlike her older sister, Muriel, May had made no attempt to cover the gray in her once bright red hair, but her eyes were the same dark blue as Jade's and vestiges of the pretty woman she'd been still lingered.

"I don't know what he sees in her," May said wistfully, gazing at the television screen. "Too good for a woman like that, he is."

Jade knew better than to ask for an explanation. To May Perron, *Coronation Street* had been realer than her life since before Jade was born. Discussions of plot lines had been known to take hours.

"Mum, I came over to ask you about something," Jade said when her mother showed signs of surfacing from her post-drama reverie. Leaving the bags of clothing behind, Jade had set out for her parents' house the moment she heard the shop door close behind Shirley.

"It's about time you remembered I'm here," May said in wounded tones. "It wouldn't hurt you to spend a bit more time with your mother. Before you know where you are, I'll be gone and then you'll wish you hadn't ignored me like you do."

"I expect you're right, Mum." Jade smiled at Ian. "How's school, then? Have you made any good friends, yet?"

"School's okay."

"A worry, he is," May said. "Our poor, dear Muriel. A saint in her own time, that's what she is."

"Perhaps Ian would enjoy poking around in the work shed. Dad's got lots—"

"Mr. Perron doesn't like strangers interfering with his things."

Jade swallowed. Her mother invariably referred to her husband as "Mr. Perron" but to Ian the comment must seem even more hostile than she'd intended.

The boy slumped lower in his chair and looked at his hands.

"Muriel's got her ramblers' meeting tonight." May sniffed and eyed Ian. "I'm just doing what anyone would do for a sister's boy. My health isn't up to it, mind, but I'm managing."

"He doesn't need . . ." Jade snapped her mouth shut, got up in a rush, and hurried across the room. *A thirteen-year-old doesn't need a baby-sitter,* she longed to say. Another moment and she'd fall into one of the pointless, one-sided arguments her mother usually won through default by silence. "I'll just pop out and see Dad."

She found her father in the greenhouse at the top of the steeply sloped garden behind the house. Tapping a pane, she leaned through the door. "Hello, Dad."

Art Perron turned from a bench crowded with potted starts and waved Jade inside. "Something gone wrong?"

"No. No, nothing like that."

"Are you sure?" Her father might be sidelined by a gammy heart but he would never stop watching Perron and Son like the anxious, first-time owner of a car in a school car park.

"Absolutely sure. Bert's ahead of schedule on

the town hall project. Gavin and Will started over in Polruan yesterday—painting the church. And Stuart's almost finished with Mrs. Graham's plastering."

"Hm." Art rotated his arthritic shoulders and arched a stooped back. "And what about you? Ferryneath, isn't it?"

Jade grinned. "Trust you, Dad. Still on top of everything."

"Got to be. No job for a woman. I still think—"

"Drop it, Dad," Jade said, but without rancor. "You know I like what I'm doing, and you also know you'd never find anyone as able as I am to run Perron's."

Art sniffed. "You'll do well to take care of things, missy. The business will be yours and your brother's when I'm gone."

"Between you and Mum, I'm glad I came over tonight," Jade said. "The pair of you. Both talking about how I'm going to feel when you die. You're both going to live for years and years yet. That's an order. Understand?"

"Hm." But a pleased smile creased Art's thin face. His pale blue eyes sparkled. Still six foot tall, despite the stiff forward thrust of his neck and narrow head, he took pride in a full head of thick, iron gray hair. He wiped his big hands on a rag and scrutinized Jade. "You never come over here on a week night. Did you fancy some sweet williams, maybe? Best in Fowey, they are. I'll cut you some."

"That'll be nice." Even if she'd probably have to resort to using milk bottles as vases. "I didn't come for that, though. Dad, we've got a problem."

Art stopped, his hands clasping the rag in front

of him. "I knew it! I should trust my instincts. You never come to see us during the week. I—"

"Dad, it's Ian."

"If Peter had come into the business the way I always planned, none of this—" He pulled his bushy brows together and slowly tossed the rag on a bench. "Ian? You mean Ada's boy?"

"Yes. Ian Spring."

"What about him? He's settling in all right, isn't he?"

"No. I don't think he is." Jade went to her father's side and slipped an arm through his. She poked at the fabric of the old painter's overalls he wore. "You were always fair, Dad. And you were always good with kids." She didn't add, especially boys—especially your favorite kid, my brother, Peter.

"Haven't had anything to do with children. Not for years."

"Don't give me that, you old sham. You're a softie for kiddies, and you know it."

"I hope I'll get to be a softie for some grandchildren of my own one day."

That, Jade decided, was a subject she didn't intend to revisit tonight, if at all. "Ian needs some help, Dad."

"Damn fool Muriel," Art muttered and snatched up a pair of pruning shears. "Damn fool woman's a menace. Thinks I should want to give up every flower in my garden for her church arrangement nonsense. She can think what she likes. I'm not giving her a stalk of anything."

"Aunt Muriel's probably trying to do her best for Ian, but she isn't young, Dad, and she's never had to do anything for a child before."

Art paused in the act of decapitating a sickly-looking geranium. "Ada left the boy to Muriel. That's the way it was arranged. No choice. He'll have to make the best of it."

"We're his family, too," Jade said patiently. "You're his uncle, and Mum's his aunt and I'm his cousin. He's lost his father and his mother and he's only thirteen. Dad, it isn't right for him to be made to feel like a nuisance."

"Feel like a nuisance?" Throwing down the shears, Art reached for the shapeless tweed hat he favored whenever outdoors. "That fool Muriel had better not make the lad feel a nuisance. I'll go over there and sort her out right now."

"No, no." Jade stood between her father and the door. "Ian's in the house with Mum. Aunt Muriel's off at her ramblers' meeting. Look, I usually avoid saying these things, but Mum defers to you. She does and says whatever she thinks you want because that's the way she believes it ought to be."

"Do you find anything wrong with that, missy?"

Jade sighed. "No, Dad. Not if it pleases you and Mum." She had long ago designated her father as a peerless chauvinist.

"If you hadn't felt you had to wear the trousers in the family, you and Doug—"

"Dad," Jade said in a mildly warning tone. "Let's stick to the reason I'm here. Mum went to Shirley Hill's shop today and bought a lot of old clothes."

Art looked blank.

"She bought them for Ian. Because Aunt Muriel asked her to."

"Why would Muriel . . . Your mother doesn't hold with secondhand things."

"I know," Jade said patiently. "And that's exactly

what I'm talking about. Evidently Mum and Aunt Muriel decided secondhand clothes are good enough for Ian even though they've never been good enough for any other member of the family. Don't you see? He's been orphaned and sent away from his home to a country halfway around the world—all in the space of a few months—and now the only family he's got is treating him like a poor relation."

"Hm." Art crammed the tweed bucket hat down to his large ears. "Hm."

"Mum was talking in front of him," Jade said, exasperated. "As if he wasn't even there. Saying Aunt Muriel's a saint to put up with having him. That sort of thing. And he isn't being allowed to behave like a boy should. I wouldn't come behind Mum's back to talk to you about something if this was a normal situation, but it isn't. And I don't know what to do to help." She spread her hands.

"D'you fancy a cuppa?" Art passed Jade and loped down the crazy paved path.

"That would be very nice." She followed, smiling to herself. The set of her father's brows suggested he would at least have something to say on the subject of Ian.

Art stopped and glanced back. "Abandoned by whoever his real mother was, too," he said, his eyebrows positively jutting. "You forgot to mention that. Don't tell me a little'un can't be scarred by what happens the minute he's born."

In her parents' immaculate kitchen, where the aroma of baking bread floated on warm air, Jade's father poured two cups of tea from a pot nestled inside a crocheted cozy atop the stove. He gave one cup to Jade, stirred four teaspoonfuls of sugar into his own, and continued wordlessly on to the living room.

Jade's mother turned her head toward her husband without removing her eyes from the television screen. "Snooker's on, Mr. Perron," she said.

"Hm."

"Get out of Mr. Perron's chair," she told Ian. "Mr. Perron's favorite, that is."

"I'm not staying," Art said, going to stand beside the boy. "Do they have humbugs in the States, then?"

Ian's brown eyes took on an even more worried glitter. "You mean phonies?"

"Thought not." Art stuffed a hand in his pocket and brought out a rumpled, white paper bag. "Humbugs are sweets. My favorites. Want one?"

Ian started to shake his head, then stood up instead and felt cautiously inside the bag until he managed to dislodge a sticky, black-and-white-striped sweet from the clump they'd formed. "Thanks," he said, turning it this way and that before edging it into his mouth.

"Good, right?"

With a pointed lump pushing out first one, then the other thin cheek, Ian nodded.

"Ever seen one of these?" From his other pocket, Art produced a dark wooden peg. "You probably have, but I'll bet you never saw someone actually make one. That's what I do for special carpentry projects. A hobby of mine. Working on a model of the *Frances of Fowey*, I am. Come on out to the shed and see."

Ian took the peg Art offered and examined it while allowing himself to be steered toward the kitchen.

"John Rashleigh's she was. Admiral Frobisher discovered Baffin Land aboard her in 1587." Man and boy disappeared and Jade heard her father add, "Went out against the Spanish Armada, too," before the door to the garden slammed shut.

"Well!" May said. "What's come over Mr. Perron? Really, it's too much. All of us having to go out of our way for a boy who isn't even related."

Jade sat in the chair Ian had vacated and cradled her teacup in both hands. "Mum, you're being too hard on Ian. You don't know him yet. Give him a chance and remember we're all he's got now."

"You don't know the half of it." May unearthed the remote control from the folds of her bathrobe, flipped off the television, and gave Jade her full attention. "That child is worrying Muriel to death. He's been seen talking to strangers."

Jade tipped her head inquiringly. "What exactly does that mean?"

"It means just exactly what I said. He's been seen talking to strange men. Now any sensible child knows better than that. He could get taken off."

The possible terrors of being "taken off" had been drummed into Jade and her older brother, Peter, from earliest memories. "I'm sure Aunt Muriel will warn him about that."

"But that's still not the half of it. He's been asking to go to one of these strangers' houses, mind you. What do you think of that?"

"I don't understand."

"No, I don't suppose you do. He reckons there's this man who's offered to give him music lessons. *Guitar*, mind you. Imagine a boy thinking he should be mucking about with guitars or whatever they are when he should be outside running about."

"As far as I can see, he isn't being encouraged to run about, or do anything else a normal thirteen-year-old should do," Jade said, almost under her breath.

"What did you say? Don't mutter to me, my girl."

"I'm thirty-two, Mum. No girl anymore. Has Ian played the guitar before?"

"I suppose so. So Muriel says, anyway. Lot of noise, I'll warrant."

Jade thought otherwise. "What's wrong with playing the guitar? I should think it would be a nice pastime for anyone."

"He wants *lessons!*" May's eyes stretched wide open. "*Imagine.* Does he think money grows on trees? Our Ada had a bit set aside to take care of the boy, but not enough for frills."

"Surely there's enough for a few extras."

"Oh, no. Our Muriel won't touch that money."

Jade slowly set her cup on a table beside the chair. "I don't understand. Aunt Muriel won't touch the money Aunt Ada left for Ian? You mean she won't use any of it for him?"

"That's exactly what I mean. Muriel's going to keep it for him so's he'll have something when he's old enough to take care of himself. She won't touch a penny. I'm not saying I completely agree, mind, but she's determined to do that for Ada even if it does mean Muriel has to scrimp a bit herself till he can go out on his own."

"Dear Auntie Muriel," Jade murmured. "She never was such a bad stick."

"What a way to talk about your aunt," May said.

"How much can guitar lessons cost?" Jade asked, ignoring her mother's admonition.

"I'm sure I don't know."

"Well, I'm going to find out. If there's someone who could teach him and it's not too expensive, I'll pay for it myself. We all need to do our bit to help Ian feel wanted." She avoided her mother's eyes. "Have you heard of anyone giving guitar lessons in Fowey or Polruan? It would be nice if he didn't have to go too far."

"No. I'm sure I haven't." May fiddled with a loose thread on the arm of her chair. "That man he met who said he'd give him lessons might be all right. But you never know, do you? A man approaching a boy like that?"

"No you don't," Jade was forced to agree. "I'll go out and see how he's getting on with Dad. Then I'll have to get home. I want to make an early start tomorrow."

Total silence met Jade when she walked into her father's work shed. On one side of a central bench, Art bent to sand a miniature plank of wood with careful and patient strokes. Ian faced Art across the bench performing the identical task with another plank.

"Good hands, he's got," Art said without glancing up. "Taking to it like a duck takes to water."

"You need good hands to play a guitar," she said, and saw the boy stiffen. "Did you know Ian plays the guitar, Dad?"

"No." Art's voice held no interest. "He says the kids at the school are nice but he doesn't fit in. They're curious about him, he says. Because he's a foreigner. But he can't fit in because he doesn't know anything about the things that interest them."

"He will. Ian, my mother's been telling me about how you want to take guitar lessons. Did you take them before?"

"Yes. Since I was eight."

"Would you like me to find someone to teach you again?" She almost held her breath. He was fragile somehow, ready to break apart if pushed too hard.

"I've found someone."

Jade stopped herself from lecturing on the evils of talking to strangers. That could come later. "Don't you think we should contact someone official? Someone who knows who's got proper credentials and so on? I could call the music teacher at the school."

"I'd like him to teach me." Ian sounded stubborn. A white line formed around his compressed lips.

"Someone you met once?" Jade asked. "A casual acquaintance? Let me—"

"I've met him lots of times . . . Several, anyway. He's nice and we know a lot of the same pieces of music. He isn't stuffy like some teachers are. We could get together and jam sometimes, too. He said so."

Jade's father had stopped sanding. He looked from Ian to Jade and shook his head slightly.

"People can say things just for something to say," she told the boy. "They often don't mean them."

"He does." Animation brought color to Ian's face. "He's resting up from his job. It's the kind that makes people tired so he's not doing it for a while. For all summer. He comes by the school in the afternoon when I'm getting out."

A tightness closed in the region of Jade's heart. "We'd better talk about this." And someone had better find out who and what this man really was. She shuddered.

"It'd be cool if I could go and visit him." Ian spoke rapidly and the flush of excitement deepened on his cheeks. "Look, he gave me this and said to have Aunt Muriel call if I can go see him."

With a hollow sickness pooling in her stomach, Jade took the piece of paper Ian gave her. "Do you think the music teacher at the school might even give lessons herself?"

Ian scuffed sawdust on the shed floor. "He understands the same things I do."

"I'm not sure—"

"Take a look at the paper," Art interrupted. "At least see where he lives. We can always check him out."

Jade nodded. "I suppose you're right. It's just that . . . Well, you know what I'm thinking." She unfolded the note and read—and read again—and again. Her skin grew tight and cold.

"Well," her father said. "Who is it? Where does he live?"

Very carefully, Jade refolded the paper. She tapped it against her chin. "Dr. Byron Frazer. Ferryneath Cottage, Bodinnick."

Chapter Eight

She was watching him again.

Byron pretended deep concentration on the papers scattered before him across the kitchen table.

But he could *feel* Jade staring at him.

He spread a hand across his brow, took off his glasses, and dangled them between a finger and thumb.

What the hell was the matter with her?

A gust of warm breeze through the open door swept in the heavy, sweet scent of honeysuckle from bushes that mounded the stone wall between the cobbled yard and an alley leading to a cottage set back from the road.

Byron settle his hand on the table and looked up in the same instant: directly into Jade Perron's cobalt blue eyes. "How's it going?" he asked.

She started, seemed to remember the can of

paint she'd presumably been stirring, and swallowed loudly enough for him to hear. "Fine," she said. Overly energetic agitation of the paint with a wooden stick ensued. Jade bowed her face over the can, which stood in the sink.

He shoved his glasses back on and opened a book.

The sluggish scraping sounds slowed, and then stopped.

Byron scanned a sentence, scanned it again— and again. To thwart a temptation to aim a sly peek at Jade, he held the book up in front of his face. She'd been the queen of frost since Wednesday. Tonight they were supposed to have a drink together and he hated to confess, even to himself, how much he looked forward to that.

She was probably trying to find a way to say she didn't intend to go.

Damn, but it shouldn't matter so much. It shouldn't matter at all. Maybe it wouldn't if he didn't feel so out of his depth and worried. Ian needed him. Every time he saw the boy, Byron searched for some sign that Ian was settling down and learning to like his surroundings. It wasn't happening.

If he took on the raising of a child, his own life would never be the same.

The words on the page ran together. From the moment he'd decided to come to Cornwall, he'd known he was opening a door he'd never intended to open again.

Ian was the child Lori had wanted so much. Smarting behind his eyes made him blink rapidly. If for no other reason than the responsibility he felt for making sure Lori's boy was happy, he no longer had a choice in what he had to do. *How* he did it was still a mystery. The doctor hadn't dealt with this particular crisis before, not in a patient, and definitely not personally. He didn't know what advice to give himself . . .

A rhythmic tapping drew his attention to the floor beside his chair. Dog—who called a dog, Dog?—sat in a contorted heap scratching an ear. When she saw him looking at her, she stopped, hind leg poised in midair, her bulbous black eyes staring him down.

"Black olives," Byron said to himself.

"What?"

He switched his attention to Jade, who gripped her dripping paint stirrer like a post hole digger— or a dagger big enough to require a two-handed thrust.

It was Byron's turn to swallow. "Dog," he said and tried, unacceptably, for a casual chuckle. "Her eyes remind me of black olives."

"She's got nice eyes. They're gentle."

"Very gentle." *Very gentle black olives.* Another strike against him. "I thought we'd go up to the Ferry Inn for a drink. Is that okay with you?"

"Oh."

Was that "oh, yes" or "oh, no"? "If you'd rather, we can find somewhere else." *But don't say you've changed your mind.*

"That'll be fine."

Fine appeared to be the word of the day. "Harry Hancock next door said it's a popular place."

"I've never been there before." She still looked less than enthusiastic. "It's expensive." An immediate and very appealing blush washed her face.

Byron pretended not to notice her comment. "Did you know Harry came from Birmingham?"

The elderly man who lived in the cottage at the end of the alley had made a point of finding excuses to talk.

"I've never met him."

"He used to drive locomotives." He wanted to talk about other things, like what she enjoyed doing when she wasn't working and what kind of books she read and what music she favored.

Jade made a neutral noise and began hauling the paint can from the sink.

Byron leaped up, almost overbalancing his chair, and went to help. "That's too heavy for you." He covered her hands on the handle.

"I'm used to lifting heavy things."

He thought he felt her tremble.

Up close, he noticed there were black flecks in the deep blue of her eyes and a hint of intense violet around each iris. "You could hurt your back," he said, his mouth unaccountably dry.

Beneath his hands, hers were small and cool. Her full lips parted a fraction. "I know how to lift properly," she said, and her attention flickered to his mouth and down to the region of the open neck of his shirt.

When she took a breath, her breasts rose beneath the shapeless white overalls that were the only mode of dress he'd seen her wear so far. She was compact, but very feminine.

"Humor me," he finally thought to say. "I'm an old-fashioned man."

Byron tightened his grip over hers and they lifted together.

"Is this going upstairs?"

"Yes."

Her skin was so pale as to be almost translucent.

Thick, black lashes created soft shadows about her eyes. Byron remembered to breathe. She was stunning in a fragile way that could be considered ludicrous in a woman with her occupation. But the steady thud, thud of his heart and the abrupt pulsing in other regions of his body had less to do with how she looked than how she made him feel.

He was aroused. He was fully, almost painfully aroused, and at the same time a weakness in his legs brought back memories of adolescent uncertainty about the next step to take with a particular woman.

"I'll carry it up for you." The paint can had become a very necessary shield. If she noticed the effect she was having on him, she'd probably run screaming from the cottage.

"I'm not ready to go up yet."

Or would she?

"Where shall I put it?" Preferably in his lap. He was seeing in her, reading in her, what he wanted to see and read.

Jade sucked her bottom lip between teeth that overlapped the tiniest bit in the front. Byron zipped through a minifantasy of running his tongue along the sharp edge of those teeth—the instant before he plunged into her mouth. While he plunged into her mouth, his hands would be full of her breasts and he would be pressing deep into her body.

"Put it back into the sink for now."

He locked his thighs. "Are you sure? I might as well take it where you're going to use it." And he could not relinquish his screen, not at this moment.

The choice wasn't to be his. "Just leave it." Her

small hands tightened under his and she guided the can to rest on its newspaper once more.

Instantly, Byron swung around, reached the table in a single stride, and dropped back into the chair. Only one other woman had ever had the power to shred his self-control—and she hadn't accomplished the process in a matter of days, or even hours, as Jade Perron had.

Jade hadn't accomplished this—he'd allowed himself to create the situation. He hated himself for comparing Lori to Jade. They were different. Period. And Ian should be his only concern. Ian was his . . . He was very concerned about Ian but any attempt to hurry things too much would probably be disastrous.

There was a great deal going on behind Jade Perron's blue eyes—a great deal more than calculating how long to stir a can of paint.

"You didn't say how the leak test went," he said.

"Nothing to panic about."

No stick for stirring paint had ever been so well cleaned. He'd swear they were equally aware of each other. This sensation of almost physical connection unnerved him. "How's it all going anyway?"

She looked questioning. "Fine."

Oh, great. Now he was repeating himself like an idiot. "I guess I already asked you that, didn't I? Sorry." With a forced laugh, he made himself pick up the book again and start reading. *"Adults who were the object of pedophilic abuse are a separate issue,"* he read yet again.

All too soon, Celeste's patience would snap again and she'd be on the phone, grilling him and refusing to go away without answers. By then he wanted a good story about his plans for the new book—a book Celeste hadn't even known he intended to write.

He grew still.

His fingers tightened on the book.

Damn it anyway. She was watching him again.

"You're really interested in all that stuff, aren't you?"

Slowly, he lowered the book. "Psychology? Yes. It's my life." It had become the only part of his life that seemed real.

"Mm. That book you're reading. It's on pedo . . . How do you say that?"

"Pedophilia."

Jade crossed her arms tightly beneath her breasts. "Something to do with children."

Byron cleared his throat. "My specialty is the family. I do a lot of inner child work. Coming to terms with needs that weren't met for people when they were children and the effect that has in later life. Adult children of addicts—alcohol, sex, violence, rage, and all the other, less obvious addictions we suffer from."

"Can not having needs met in early life cause something like pedophilia? How would you explain exactly what that is, anyway?"

The intense expression in her eyes troubled him. "In simplest terms, pedophilia is a sexual perversion in which children are the preferred sexual object." He felt surprisingly uncomfortable.

Jade shuddered. "That's awful."

"It's a disease. Like any other disease."

"I think it's disgusting."

He wouldn't give her a lecture on treating deviations rather than banishing those who suffered from them. "It's a problem."

She crossed her arms even tighter and came closer. The neck of her overalls was unbuttoned to a point where her breasts pressed together and a dark line of shadow formed. He shifted in his chair.

"Is it true that some people—not you of course—but some people go into fields like . . . Well, do they choose things to solve their own problems?"

Byron affected careful consideration. She couldn't know that the question was one of the oldest in the book. "Like mixed-up psychologists?"

She put a finger on top of one of his sheets of notes and pushed it gently back and forth. "Maybe. Do you think a person can cure himself of some serious psychological deviation?"

He had no idea where she was heading. "It's possible."

"But not usual?"

"Sometimes conditions are dormant for long periods. That frequently ends up causing the biggest problem because the subject builds a normal reputation. Whatever 'normal' is. And when the deviation eventually starts to kick in, the subject is often intelligent enough to camouflage his or her anomaly pretty well."

"But they won't be able to forever?" She pulled up a chair and sat close to Byron. Too close. "Sooner or later they're going to start acting out their fantasies."

He raised his eyebrows sharply. "Fantasies? What makes you zero in on fantasies?"

"Oh, nothing. It was just a word." She leaned toward him, watching his face so closely he wanted to look away. "What happens when they can't suppress the, er, whatever it is anymore?"

"There aren't any absolutes. Sometimes the behaviors come on gradually. Sometimes there's a rush. The trick is to recognize what's happening and head off disaster."

"Oh, yes. I'm sure no pedophilic person wants to take off children."

"Take off?"

Jade became a mass of agitated movement. "Take off. You know. Lure away by offering them things. Single out a boy who looks lonely and promise him whatever he wants most and then get him to go somewhere. That kind of thing."

To the contrary, Byron knew that in many instances pedophiles had no compunction about pursuing their urges. He wasn't about to upset Jade with that piece of information. "We can certainly hope that may be the case," he told her. "You really like children, don't you?"

"Well . . . I do like them, yes. Byron, there's something I'd like to discuss with you."

The tone of her voice made his scalp feel too small. "Discuss away." Why did he sense he wasn't going to enjoy this?

"I don't want you to think I'm not sympathetic, because I am, but I can't risk keeping my mouth shut and regretting it later. Not that my regret is the important issue."

"I'm used to talking openly on just about any subject. If I can help put your mind at ease about something, I want to."

"It's about, well—"

"Morning." Harry Hancock leaned his stocky body in at the kitchen door. "Thought you might enjoy a piece of my bread pudding. I'm not interrupting anything, am I?"

Chapter Nine

Byron passed the bathroom in the upstairs hall. Dog sat outside the door waiting for her mistress. The dog looked at Byron and drew her lips away from her teeth in what Jade referred to as a smile. Byron wasn't sure he and Dog were on smiling terms.

When she'd finished work, Jade had asked, hesitantly, if she could "wash and brush up" before they had their drink. Then she'd produced a plastic grocery sack from the room where she'd been working. Even though it was larger, she had declined his offer to use the bathroom off his bedroom. And she hadn't met his eyes when she'd said, "That isn't necessary." He hovered at the top of the stairs and smiled. Perhaps he wasn't the only one around here who was feeling some sexual stirrings.

The lock clicked off on the bathroom door.

Byron slipped silently downstairs and into the

sitting room. Without putting on the light, he sat on the couch where he could see Jade pass by in the hall and enter the kitchen that lay straight ahead in his line of sight.

He felt his own pulse, strong and heavy—and excited.

This wasn't just an almost forgotten feeling, it was a first in the intensity department.

Her footsteps came softly down the stairs and she walked past the sitting room door—and stood still, looking toward the kitchen.

With her back to him, she looked down and her movements suggested she was checking buttons on her blouse.

Byron leaned forward and rested his elbows on his knees. The pulsing in his veins became a throb. Whatever he'd expected, it hadn't been quite the curvaceous figure in a yellow blouse, simple, tapered black slacks, and flat black shoes who hovered, spotlighted, mere yards from him.

Jade Perron couldn't be classified as a butterfly emerged from a chrysalis. That she was intriguing, he already knew. But an intriguing face with the promise of more had emerged as a totally feminine and elegant presence who had managed to shake this worldly male to the soles of his Ferragamo loafers.

Keeping her arms at her sides, she walked on and disappeared into the kitchen. Dog moved like a shadow in her wake.

Byron got up. *Damn it.* He hadn't come here to get involved with a woman, but he had a notion that might be about to happen. All day Ian had been heavy on his mind. The time had come to make a final decision in that area, and Byron thought he might be ready to do just that. But for tonight, Jade of the freckled white skin and blue eyes, of the thick black hair with a mind of its own, the minuscule waist—and fascinating breasts—yeah, she was the main item on the agenda tonight. He wanted to know more about her, to understand more about her.

Anchoring his hands in the pockets of his slacks with what he hoped was a nonchalant air, he strolled in to confront her. "Hi. I thought maybe we'd be daring and have a drink here before we go out. Ready to be wowed by Byron the bartender?"

Sitting on top of a step stool, with one obviously shapely leg crossed over the other, she turned her face up to his and said, "Why not? I've clocked out. Now I feel reckless."

In that instant, all his years of experience in the noble art of smoothly negotiating the dating dance wobbled dangerously. "What will you have?"

"Whatever you're having."

She'd brushed her hair until it shone like blue-black satin, and drawn it back on one side with a plain ebony comb. He'd never liked red lipstick. On Jade, the unexpected effect acted like a magnet. He wanted to feel that full, soft, carmine-tinted mouth beneath his own. "Do you like wine?" he asked.

"That's fine."

No way would he allow her to retreat into that line of response. He said, "Red or white," and almost laughed at himself for giving her the perfect opportunity to say, "Either."

Instead, she said, "You choose." And she swung a foot, allowing the heel of her shoe to dangle. Her ankles were narrow. Everything about her felt like something he was noticing for the first time in a woman—as if he'd never noticed anything in particular about a woman before.

He drew in a breath and retreated to grab a bottle of red wine from a rack on the counter . . . and to regroup. They were going to have a drink, exchange a few pleasantries, and then she'd go home.

"You chose red," she said when he handed her a glass.

"Seems appropriate." Like the color of her lips. "What shall we drink to?"

She looked directly into his eyes. "I'm not much good at toasts."

"Try." And let him keep right on looking at her—until he could figure out a way to touch what he was looking at. Geez, he was thinking like the kind of man he'd never wanted to be—an on-the-make-at-any-cost man.

"How about, here's to hope, and honesty and generosity and kindness and"—she wrinkled her nose thoughtfully—"and you finish."

"Finish?" He grimaced. "You're a tough act to follow. I'll just throw in friendship. How's that?"

She held up her glass and waited for him to touch it with his own. "That's just about perfect." Crystal tapped her white teeth and she sipped.

Watching her covertly, Byron took a deep swallow of his own drink. The blouse was made of silk and settled lightly on her breasts. She balanced the wineglass on her knee and turned it by the stem. The blouse was thin. She wore a pale, lacy bra that didn't reach much higher than her nipples. Soft flesh flared above the lace.

"You're staring."

He jumped, actually *jumped*. "Not staring. Thinking and gazing. There's a difference." At least his ability to think on his feet hadn't deserted him.

"What are you thinking?"

"That I'm not sure drinking in a pub with a lot of people is what I want to do." Good God! He rarely spoke without thinking first, but he'd just done exactly that. "But I can be a bit reclusive, so don't take any notice of me. I'll enjoy myself the minute we get there."

"I'd rather not go either."

He paused, the glass halfway to his mouth.

"I've never been very fond of noisy places." She shrugged—the most charming shrug he ever remembered seeing. "It's fun to think about going somewhere. But when the time comes to leave, I always feel a bit sick. Isn't that silly?" She tilted her head self-consciously and flipped her hair back from her neck, a slender, pale neck that carried on down to an equally pale, smooth expanse of skin exposed between the lapels of her blouse.

Byron's brain clicked sluggishly back into gear. "I don't find anything about you silly." *Whoa, boy. The water could quickly get deeper than you're prepared to dive in to.* "How do you feel about being all dressed up with nowhere to go?"

"I already am somewhere." She turned the delightful shade of pink he'd already decided he could find addictive. "I mean, it's nice being able to relax and do nothing . . . in nice surroundings . . . with someone . . ."

Byron laughed. "Someone nice?"

"I was going to say 'different.' But nice, too."

The way she blushed shouldn't please him this much. He said, "Why don't we have something to eat? It's that time."

After a pause, she said, "Why don't I fix something?"

"You're sure you don't want to go out?"

"Absolutely sure now." She slid to stand, with the result that for a moment her slacks pulled tight around her thighs.

As far as he could tell, she had perfect legs and he'd like nothing more than to run his hands up their length, all the way up their length.

Moments later, Jade's head was buried in the refrigerator, which meant that her small, but wonderfully rounded bottom was presented for inspection.

A shudder passed all the way to his toes. This was getting out of hand. There'd never been a doubt in his mind that he was a sexual animal, but his reaction to Jade went way beyond the expected.

"We could use this as an excuse to clean out your refrigerator," she said from its recesses. "You've got bits and pieces of just about everything."

Byron moved behind her. "Sounds great. Hand out the booty and I'll put it on the table."

She started to pass containers and packages to him, then said, "That's about it," stood, and closed the door.

"Hardly a gourmet repast," Byron said.

Jade turned. She stood almost toe to toe with him, her chin tipped up. "It'll fill us up."

He made no attempt to move away.

Neither did Jade.

Unable to stop himself, Byron pushed the fingers of one hand into her hair and used his thumb to outline a high, rounded cheekbone.

Jade passed her tongue over her lips, and the light in her eyes became a glitter that turned them black. "I'll put everything on a tray," she said in a voice that broke. "Shall we eat here? Or in the sitting room, where we can watch it get dark over the harbor?"

"And the lights go on across the water," Byron said, shifting his thumb to her bottom lip and brushing lightly back and forth. "The water shifts under the reflections. It seems endless and bottomless and so soft." And it reminded him of the lady who stood before him.

"So it'll be the sitting room?"

"Uh-huh." Reluctantly, he removed his hand and helped put cheese and meat and an odd assortment of fruit onto plates.

By the time they'd arranged their eclectic feast on the low table in the sitting room, the charged atmosphere between them had relaxed. Byron didn't know if he was relieved. Scratch that. He was almost damned sure he *wasn't* relieved.

"The light in here makes it hard to see the harbor," Jade said, carrying a plate and her glass of wine to a padded seat in the window.

Byron flipped the switch that turned off the overhead light and killed the room's two lamps. "Now I suppose we won't be able to see to eat."

Jade giggled. He never remembered hearing her giggle before. "I could get food into my mouth if you sewed it shut. Ask my mother."

"That's it," he blurted out. "That's what's so different about you."

When he reached her side, carrying a glass and plate of his own, he saw the sheen of her eyes as she looked up at him. "What's different? I'm very ordinary. A working woman with a business to run."

"But you don't take yourself seriously. And you're perfectly comfortable with who you are. Do you know how rare that is? I can't remember the last time I met a woman who didn't seem to be considering the impression she made."

"Who has time? You aren't worrying about the impression you make on me either, are you?"

"No." Not entirely true.

"So we're even."

His next thought was less pleasing. It was very doubtful that Jade Perron had any idea who he was in professional terms. If she did, she'd probably go into the posting, designed-to-attract routine to which he was so accustomed. She absolutely did not know why he was in Cornwall. The idea brought him discomfort. He hadn't told her any lies, but neither had he given her even a hint of the truth about himself.

She carefully balanced her food and wine and pulled her feet beneath her on the seat. Darkness had finally become almost complete, and the harbor waters rose and fell beneath bands of wavering lights from buildings overhanging the river on the Fowey side.

"Have you lived here all your life?" he asked her. Suddenly it seemed very important to know much more about Jade.

"Yes. And my father and mother before me and their parents before them and on and on back for generations."

"And you love it."

"I don't think about it a lot, but yes, I'm fond of Fowey."

"You said you live over a secondhand shop."

"On Lostwithiel Street. New to You, it's called. It belongs to Shirley Hill. Her husband is Sam Hill, who runs one of the water taxi services."

"Do they live in the same building?"

"Next door. Sam's family's been here a long time, too. He owns several pieces of real estate in town."

"Do you have a—er—flat mate? Is that what you call it here?" And would she please manage not to notice that he was prying?

"Flat mate's the right thing. No, I live alone—except for Dog." The animal had remained in the kitchen, asleep in a corner. "We make a great team. I give all the orders. She follows most of them and never answers back. Which makes me the boss."

"And being the boss is important to you."

"It becomes important to people who have lived with tyrants who . . ." Her voice trailed off.

"You've lived with a tyrant?"

"That's finished. It was a long time ago."

In other words: *Back off.*

"How about you?" she asked. "Back in Tiburon? Do you have someone?"

Byron's heart missed a beat. He drank more wine and refilled his glass. He made a production of matching chunks of cheese to crackers.

"Is that yes? I only asked because you asked me first."

He took a slice of pear from his plate and offered it to her. "Do you like these? I don't." When she'd accepted the fruit, he continued, "I tend to think about what I'm going to say for too long. Probably one more occupational idiosyncracy. I live alone. Don't even have a dog. I'm not married." Saying it aloud gave him the sensation of being punched in the stomach. He probably ought to say he had been married, but he didn't want to explain what had happened to Lori—or think about it yet again.

Jade drank thoughtfully. "You surprise me. I'd have thought by your . . . Well, most men of your . . . I never was very good at nosing around without sounding rude."

"I'm thirty-four." And it was time for a change of subject. "This morning, when Harry Hancock came by, you were about to ask me something. You never got around to finishing."

Selecting a square of Cheddar cheese, Jade put it in her mouth and munched for several seconds. "Mm. I don't remember what it was now. Harry's a nice man. Kind."

"And wise," Byron told her while an absolute conviction formed that she definitely had not forgotten whatever it was she'd wanted to say. "After you went back to work, he said you were beautiful."

Jade shook her head and turned her face to the window. "That's nice. I am surprised you haven't been married."

Evasion could only drag him into a tighter and tighter spot. "I have been married."

"To a woman?"

He almost dropped his glass. "I beg your pardon?"

"Oh, dear. No, that's not what I meant." She

shifted and put her plate on the windowsill. "What happened? I mean . . . Oh, dear."

Yet again he had the unpleasant sensation that something quite different from what she presented was on Jade's mind. "My wife died. I was twenty-one. She was twenty." Why, when he never, ever discussed Lori, had he felt forced to bare the truth to a woman who was little more than a stranger?

"That's awful," Jade whispered. "How sad. God rest her soul. I'm very sorry, Byron. What happened?"

No. Now he must tread very carefully. "She had an aneurysm. Two, actually. After the first there seemed some hope, but then the second one happened and it was all over." For a while—for months— he'd thought his life was over too.

Jade found his hand in the gloom and pressed his fingers. "Sometimes I think allowing yourself to love is too dangerous."

"Why?" He wasn't ready to ask about the past she had very clearly shared with someone, some man.

"Because when things go wrong, or break apart, at least one of you is left in pain. The pain makes you feel you want to die. Then the pain goes, but it takes your trust with it and I'm not sure you ever get that back completely."

Silence filled in around them. Byron had the uncanny sensation she could see into his soul— and that, just maybe, he had a glimpse into hers. He could come to like Jade's soul a great deal.

"I suppose that kind of personal disaster could affect a person in all sorts of strange ways," she said at last. "Did it . . . did it affect you in strange ways, do you think?"

He thought about that. "I think it made me wary of going into the expected types of relationships again." An understatement.

"Mm. I know that's true." She scooted a little closer. "What made you come so far away from home?"

Once again an edginess crept into his brain. "It seemed like a good idea. Sometimes we all need a complete break with what's going on, and a chance to assess our lives."

"I see. But was there a specific reason for coming?"

She definitely had something on her mind, but this time she wouldn't find out what she wanted to know. He'd try not to tell an outright lie, but he couldn't risk mentioning Ian. "What do you mean," he said, "a specific reason?"

"Ooh, I don't know." Her next breath was uneven. "Like . . . Like some kind of trouble you wanted to get away from, maybe?"

Byron reached down and set both his glass and plate on the floor. His stomach had executed a perfect backflip. "Trouble?" he asked carefully. "What sort of trouble?"

"Well . . . *trouble.* You know, something that made you feel like going a long way away and starting afresh, I suppose."

He regarded her narrowly in the darkness, an idea forming that caused a mixture of confusion, and deep anger. "Do you think I'm a fugitive from the law, for God's sake?"

"No! No, of course not. Whatever would give you an idea like that? I'm so bad at expressing myself." She raised her wrist to her nose and peered at her watch. "My word, if I don't hurry, I'll miss the last ferry. They stop so early. I don't want to have to call for the water taxi."

Byron felt disoriented. "You didn't bring your van?"

"No. Because we were having dinner, I decided to come over as a passenger."

"But you haven't finished your dinner—such as it is. Stay. I'll drive you around."

"Oh, no. I've got to get on or I won't be worth anything in the morning. I want to get started early on the ceiling in that bedroom. Things seem to be taking me longer than I expected."

He forced himself not to say that he'd been hoping he could find a way to keep her here all summer.

In a flurry, she transported their barely touched repast to the kitchen, rushed upstairs to gather the bag she'd left in the bathroom, and made to leave.

"Hey," Byron said. "Hold on. We've got ten minutes yet and the ferry stops practically at the edge of the garden. Give me the bag and I'll walk you down."

Side by side, they walked downhill past the front of Ferryneath to the landing. In the distance, on the other side of the water, Byron could see that the ferry had yet to cast off and chug in their direction.

"Can we do this again?" he asked. There was much more about Ms. Perron that would probably be very engrossing to discover.

"You want to?" Surprise loaded her words.

He wanted to turn her into his arms, to kiss her until they were both breathless.

The timing was wrong.

"I want to. I think I want to get to know you, Jade. Maybe very well. Does that sound like something that would interest you?"

She turned toward him and looked up into his face. With a single knuckle, she tapped his chest repeatedly. "You confuse me. Yes, it would interest me. It might even interest me a lot. But there are things we'd have to get straight first."

"Such as?"

"I'm not in the market for a casual lover."

Just like that? Byron recovered fast. "Casual lovers have never been my thing."

"There's something more important than that."

"Fire away."

"I—" Abruptly, she swung away and stood with her back to him.

"You what?" Her moods swept back and forth like a crazed pendulum. His tendency had been to avoid bringing his profession into his private relationships, but this lady was beginning to rattle him. "Jade, what is it? You've made several comments that could be classified as strange. Would it be too much to ask you to tell me what's really on your mind?"

"I don't like this. I don't like it one bit."

The ferry barge's engine blossomed to a full rumble that echoed over the water. "Okay," Byron said, fueled by a sense of urgency. "Would you please tell me what it is? I can take it, I assure you."

Stooping, she hauled Dog into her arms and turned to Byron once more. Even in the darkness, he could see anxiety in her eyes. "I've got to ask you why you've been following Ian Spring around."

Everything inside him plummeted. He pivoted

on a heel, shoved his hands in his pockets, and looked at her over his shoulder. "Hell. This is a small town and no doubt it has a small-town mentality—in other words, you all live in one another's pockets. But how in God's name do you know I've been talking to Ian?"

"You've been waiting for him outside school and talking to him."

The ferry's engine became a rapidly approaching roar. "I'm not denying that. But you owe it to me to explain how you know."

"I don't owe you anything. You offered to give him guitar lessons and he wants to come."

He laughed without mirth. "This takes the cake. Okay. Yes. Guilty as charged. I asked Ian to come to the cottage and jam. I play the guitar, too. And I'll give him a hand with technique as much as I can. If he's allowed to come."

"Answer my question, Byron. Why?"

For one insane instant he considered doing just that. The urge passed. "I like the boy. We met in the churchyard and discovered we were both Americans. I thought he was lonely and I was right. Put it down to my occupation. I've spent a lot of time analyzing people." If his excuse sounded as phony to her as it did to him, he could expect a lot more questioning. He breathed into a fist, willing the clamoring in his mind to quit. He said, "Do you believe me?"

Jade stared straight into his eyes. "Maybe."

"Maybe? Okay, I guess that's something. Now. How about you telling me where you get your intelligence on Ian and me?" He passed his tongue over dry lips. "And what gives you the right to interfere anyway?"

"His mother was Ada Spring," Jade said quietly.

Byron let his hands fall to his sides. "I'll let you finish before I ask how you know that." And however long she took to finish would be too long.

"Cornish people believe in sticking by family. We don't let anything get in the way of that. I won't pretend I don't enjoy your attention, Byron. I'll even admit that—to quote a certain friend of mine's terminology—you turn me on."

He found his mouth open and closed it. "The feeling's mutual." But he wasn't accustomed to quite such a blunt, matter-of-fact approach.

How did she know about Ada Spring, dammit, how did she know?

"Ada Spring married an American and went to live in the States. They couldn't have children, so they adopted Ian. Only now they're both dead and he was sent here to Cornwall to live with Muriel Cadwen. Ada Spring was her sister."

The possible instigator of this came to light. Ian must have mentioned Byron to his aunt, and Muriel set about spreading gossip about his intentions toward the boy.

"That's why I've got a responsibility toward Ian. Muriel Cadwen is my aunt. She's my mother's sister. Ada Spring was also my mother's sister."

Byron splayed a hand over his face. He couldn't think of a thing to say.

"The fact is that if you've decided to make things harder for my Aunt Muriel by unsettling Ian, I'll find a way to stop you.

"Ian Spring is my cousin."

Chapter Ten

The cottage seemed to be holding its breath. Jade rose to tiptoe and climbed the stairs with exaggerated steps. Byron was usually up and already at work when she arrived in the early morning. Today there was no sign of him, which probably meant he'd gone out somewhere. He had a Land Rover and parked it farther up the lane, in an old stable yard where they rented spaces. She could have checked before coming into the cottage. But just in case he was still sleeping, she'd try to be as quiet as possible.

She hesitated. After the questions she'd asked him last night, and the suggestions she'd made, he could have decided to leave. The breathlessness she felt had nothing to do with climbing a few stairs. *Don't let him be gone.*

If he was, it would be because he had something

to escape from—like being discovered as a child molester.

The next steps Jade took were even slower than those that had gone before. She hadn't had enough sleep and she'd been up since three. First she'd wondered if she should come at all, then she'd waited for the phone to ring—for a message telling her she should not go to Ferryneath until further notice.

The door to his bedroom stood open a few inches, and dim light beyond suggested the curtains were still closed.

Wincing at the creak of a floorboard, she crept on past to the second bedroom and took off the old parka she'd donned against an unexpectedly cold fog that had rolled in during the night.

The time she'd spent talking to Byron was all a confused and vaguely embarrassing jumble now. If she didn't have an obligation to get on with the job, she probably wouldn't have come this morning.

The walls in this room had been stripped of old paper and she'd almost finished rough-plastering the ceiling between beams the owners had agreed to leave exposed—thanks to the good word Byron had put in for her idea.

She rolled up her sleeves and bent to pry the lid from a can of clear stain.

A scraping noise snapped her attention to Dog, who was tugging her favorite hammer from the upper tray of Jade's toolbox.

"Ssh," she warned. "Leave it!"

The lid on the can of stain popped off.

Dog, one eye on Jade, gave the hammer another yank and brought the head clattering to the bare floor. The handle remained gripped in bared teeth.

"Naughty!" Jade lowered her voice. "Naughty girl. You drop it."

Dog obliged.

Jade jumped at the ensuing racket and sucked air in through her teeth.

She waited, listening for sounds of movement from the room next door. None came.

Beyond the uncurtained windows, fog billowed so thick, the river was obscured. From the south, in the direction of St. Austell Bay, came the sonorous cry of foghorns.

A miserable morning, Jade decided. A morning when it would be nice to pull the covers over one's head and remain in bed—like the fortunate Dr. Frazer was probably doing right now.

Dr. Frazer—tall, hair ruffled, powerful arms and legs thrown wide, face undoubtedly handsomely boyish in sleep—stretched out on the bed beyond the wall she faced . . . Thoughts such as these did not make for serene working conditions.

A scraping sound forced her attention precipitously back to Dog who, dragging the wretched hammer, disappeared rapidly into the upstairs hallway.

Jade set down the screwdriver she'd used to pry the lid off the stain can, and scurried after the animal.

Too late.

She arrived just in time to see a long, scrawny, almost hairless tail disappear into Byron Frazer's bedroom. The hammer, apparently less interesting than whatever had grabbed Dog's attention, lay on the floor outside.

"Dog," Jade hissed, bending low and creeping forward until she stood close to the six-inch opening into Byron's room. "Dog, get out here."

Rustling followed and the distinctive sound of Dog's yawn. Then nothing.

"Dog!" She covered her face and tried to think what to do. Byron had never shown any particular fondness for her pet. If he awakened to find her in his room, he might insist that Jade leave her behind in future. "Dog, *come* here." Dog was misunderstood by others. Nobody but Jade knew what a gentle, faithful friend she was.

Hovering anxiously, Jade put a forefinger on the door and pushed, waited, and pushed again, widening the space until she could risk putting enough of her head inside to peer into the gloom beyond.

The bed stood against the wall between two windows; "looking as if a tornado had struck" didn't cover the twisted mess of quilt and sheets heaped on top and trailing to the floor.

Byron hadn't gone anywhere.

Dog, grinning as only Dog could grin, sat nestled in the space between Byron's splayed feet. The evil animal might have short legs, but they always got her where she wanted to go.

As Jade watched, her mutt's long, pink tongue appeared and toured in a leisurely lick from the man's heel, over his instep, to his big toe.

And one of those long, powerful legs Jade had been visualizing jackknifed up.

She covered her mouth and started to withdraw, but the fresh assault on the bed's covers ceased as abruptly as it had begun.

"Come here," Jade mouthed to Dog, making extravagant hand signals. *"Now!"*

Still grinning, her tongue lolling out of her mouth, Dog stood, turned around and around and around, then flopped down and closed her eyes.

Grimly determined, Jade bowed lower and advanced like the Grinch about to lift a little Who's candy cane on Christmas Eve.

Dog opened one eye, and scootched until she curled into the dark hollow beside Byron's other leg.

Common sense suggested it was a fine time to retreat and wait for the feathers to hit the fan. A lifelong tendency to try for the impossible if there was the slightest chance of triumph sent Jade treading softly onward until she was beside Byron.

"Dog," she whispered.

Her answer was the sliding progress of a bump that shimmied along the outline of the man's leg—*under* the covers.

Jade planted her hands on her hips.

And she looked at the man. She looked at him with her eyes wide open, and what felt like a fist in her throat.

He was spectacular.

He was breathtaking.

He was the sexiest thing she'd set eyes on . . . ever.

And how right her little fantasy had been. Very tall, one powerful arm folded beneath his head, strongly muscled legs flung wide, dark curly hair tousled . . . face handsomely boyish and relaxed in sleep . . . all just about as she'd visualized.

Something drew her even closer. Something in her, and something in him.

The night's growth of beard was dark on his angular jaw. And his lashes flickered with the movement of his closed eyes. Why hadn't she noticed how thick those lashes were?

He shifted and the bedding underwent another attack. Everything slid until only his hips, anchoring a swathe of sheet, kept the entire mess from landing on the floor.

Byron's right arm swung toward Jade and his hand came to rest, palm up, scant inches from her hip.

Drawing in a deep breath that wedged in her throat, she allowed her gaze to travel from Byron's face in a downward direction.

His shoulders were wide and well muscled, and tanned.

His chest was beautifully defined, the pectorals smooth and each rib covered with toned flesh—and tanned. Dark, curly hair flared wide, then gradually tapered to a line past his navel, and flared again . . . all the way to the twisted band of white sheet.

She'd seen his bare torso and legs before, but not like this, not while he lay before her.

His thighs were solid and well shaped, and his calves, and fine, dark hair lay smoothly on the skin—tanned skin.

His . . . Jade almost let out a small cry. Her hand went to her throat. At this moment, Byron Frazer was one hard man and he had plenty of raw material ready to prove exactly how hard.

"Do you know what they call people who do what you're doing?"

At the rasp of Byron's voice, Jade jumped violently.

His hand closed on her wrist, stopping her from rushing out of the room.

He drew her even closer to the bed until her thighs pressed against the mattress. "They call them voyeurs," he said.

"Dog," she croaked, and coughed. "Dog came in here and I tried to get her out."

In the silvered light of early morning, the man's eyes took on the quality of still, deep water—clear green all the way to some shifting place no one might see.

"I was working in the other room," Jade said. His grip on her wrist didn't waver. "Dog took off and . . ." He wasn't listening.

Her pesky mutt chose that moment to scramble from the bed and scuttle out of the room.

Byron's concentration remained right where it had been—on Jade. "You're a very sensual woman. But you know that, don't you?"

She expanded her chest, but no air filled her lungs.

"Don't you?" He shook her arm slightly.

She moistened her dry lips. "I should go."

"Do you want to?"

Jade made herself look away. "I've still got several weeks of work to do here, Byron. Maybe we should forget last night ever happened . . . and this morning."

"And that's what you want?" he persisted.

"No." Her small voice sounded distant, as if it belonged to someone else.

"I didn't think so. Neither do I. And I think this

is as good a time as any to get rid of a few doubts you've had about me."

"Doubts?" Still she didn't trust herself to look at him.

"Poor Jade. You really did intend to do battle with me over Ian, didn't you?"

A dull heat crept up her neck. "You can't blame me for being concerned about what I was told. When grown men approach little boys outside schools, certain conclusions are inevitable."

"I told you the truth. I met Ian. He's a lonely kid and I wanted to help him. That's part of what I do for a living. Help people who are hurting. Do you believe me?"

"Yes." She meant it.

He fell silent. His fingers gentled on her wrist. She could have pulled away. She didn't want to.

Byron began to rub his thumb back and forth over the soft skin on the inside of her wrist. With his fingers, he played feathery touches into her palm.

Neither of them moved.

"Kiss me, Jade."

She closed her eyes. Her knees weakened and she fought against the desire to kneel beside him.

A little tug jerked her forward. "Please. I've been dreaming about your mouth. I've dreamed about feeling your lips part on mine, and about tasting you. I've wanted to push my tongue between your teeth and have you do the same to me."

She looked into his eyes. She had to. The green was more emerald now, intense and glittering.

"I've dreamed about you awake and asleep."

"I'm nobody," she whispered. "A woman who does a job with her hands and goes home to an empty little flat—to no one. I've failed in a relationship, Byron. I promised myself I wouldn't get close enough to anyone to feel a repeat of the kind of hurt that brought me." She couldn't handle this so she might as well get out without even getting in.

He raised his chin and smiled, deepening the dimpled grooves beside his mouth and crinkling the lines at the corners of his eyes. "And you can feel we might have a relationship that would make you vulnerable again?"

She said, "Yes," while she hated the admission.

"Good. It's healthy to be able to get involved again."

"Is it?"

"Kiss me." His white teeth pressed into his bottom lip and he pulled her steadily down until she must either give in or withdraw and turn away from him. "Do to me what I've dreamed of, Jade. And let me do the same for you."

His other hand went around her neck and he lifted his head from the pillow. There was the briefest instant, a tiny beat in time before he urged their mouths together.

Softly, so softly, his lips grazed over Jade's. Back and forth, back and forth, and somewhere in the gentle caressing of skin on skin, the tip of his tongue slipped between her teeth, and withdrew again.

Jade's eyes closed. Only Byron's hands stopped her from falling onto the bed with him. He kissed her with his lips, his tongue, tracing the tender, moist skin just inside her mouth until it tingled, teasing her tongue to join his, then pulling away yet again, leaving her lips swollen and wanting.

In a single movement, he knelt on the bed and wrapped his arms around Jade's waist. "This is too fast."

She nodded, fighting for breath. "I know."

"Sometimes things happen that we couldn't have planned if we'd wanted to. Do you believe that?"

"Yes." Her body felt raw.

"This scares you."

"I'm not impulsive, Byron. It scares me."

"Which makes you very wise. Would you believe me if I said it scares me, too?"

She thought a moment, all the while staring back at him. "I believe you."

"That kiss wasn't enough. Not for me."

Her heart slammed in her chest.

"I need much more, Jade."

She glanced down. The sheet had entirely given up its task. "You want . . ." She laughed shortly. "What a stupid thing I almost said."

"That I want sex? I do, Jade. But with you. Only with you."

"Nothing like this has ever happened to me before."

"And you're thinking it's happened to me?" His hands began a rough, shaky massage up and down her back. "Maybe you even think it's happened often. It hasn't. Not ever. I live a quiet life. There's no one else, Jade. There hasn't been for a very long time." And he cupped her bottom, urged her so near, she braced her hands on his shoulders.

"We're grown-ups," he murmured. "We don't owe explanations to anyone."

"No."

"And it's a cool, foggy day out there." Very slowly, he first spanned her waist, then ran his hands up her arms to her shoulders. "In here it's warm and safe and private—and we can be and do whatever we want for as long as we want. Tell me what you want."

All she could do was swallow hard and watch his face.

Byron kept his eyes on hers and unbuttoned the top button on her overalls.

Jade's hand instantly covered his and she shook her head.

"Okay." He smiled. "Okay, sweetheart. At least stay with me until I get myself back together."

She bowed her head and removed her hand from his. "I don't want you to stop."

He didn't.

The button slipped from its hole, and the next, and the next, until he could spread open the top of the overalls.

"My God," he murmured. "You're going to make me explode."

With the very tips of his fingers, he passed along the strip of narrow satin ribbon where her breasts swelled over the cups of a brief, peach-colored bra.

Jade watched his tanned fingers linger where the wisp of satin didn't cover the arcs of her dusky nipples. He leaned to kiss her there, lightly, moving his head languorously from side to side. She inhaled and closed her eyes against a longing for him to do much more.

Byron slid the overalls from her shoulders and down her arms, waiting until she pulled her hands free before framing her face and taking his time over another long kiss.

The muscles in his arms flexed beneath her fingers. Her hair fell forward to tumble over his shoulders.

Slowly, he ended the kiss and pressed his lips to her brow, her closed eyes, her neck.

"You smell like roses," he murmured. "I noticed that last night."

"I want to forget last night."

"I don't want to forget anything about the time I spend with you."

The time. She recognized the implied limit. Whatever happened between them would be bounded by the length of his stay in Cornwall.

Then he would be gone . . .

"Jade?" His voice held a question.

She looked into his face. "Yes."

"I can feel you drawing away. I don't want this to be something you're going to regret."

Finally unable to control the shaking in her legs, Jade leaned against the side of the bed. "I'm never going to regret it," she told him and knew she was probably lying.

The backs of his fingers passed from her collarbones down to the incredibly sensitized edges of her nipples . . . and dipped beneath the plunging bra.

Jade watched his face, the rigid set of his jaw, the intense concentration in his eyes. Byron watched her body's response.

He unhooked the fastening between her breasts

nd brushed aside the flimsy garment. Her nipples hardened.

Byron stroked her shoulders. And while his eyes
flickered over her, he covered her breasts, held
them, pressed them together, and finally, lavished
each one with long, dragging kisses that drew her
nipples far into his mouth.

Heat and aching flashed from his lips, his
tongue, his teeth, to bury themselves deep inside
her.

Byron's mouth never left her, not while he
stripped her naked, not when he clamped her between his legs, holding her against his rock-hard
erection with the relentless force of a vise.

Time and sanity crowded together.

They did not speak.

Byron tipped Jade backward onto the bed and
bent over her thighs. With his tongue he found his
way through dark hair to pulsing flesh, and sent
her into hot darkness where the only sounds were
her cry and his murmurs of satisfaction.

When she pushed him away and rolled to stand
on the floor again, he knelt once more and tried
to pull her back onto the bed. Jade went to her
knees. She slid her hands up his thighs. When she
cradled him, caressed him again and again, she
heard his harsh breathing, then a wild cry of ec-
stasy—and of surrender.

And when Byron swept her up and deposited
her in the middle of his big, tumbled bed, only
Jade's muffled whimper and Byron's groan accompanied his entry into her.

In the rush of motion, the sounds they made
mingled. Jade arched her hips from the bed, and

Byron did what neither of them could have stopped—or would have stopped.

With the last, releasing thrust, he fell, panting, on top of her. His hot, damp skin slipped over hers. He found her hands and stretched her arms above her head, laced their fingers together and rested his face in her neck.

Even as they lay there, breathless and exhausted, Byron's knee moved rhythmically up and down the inside of Jade's thigh.

She wriggled, trying to get more comfortable.

"Don't do that," he said against her shoulder. "Not unless you're ready to repeat what we obviously do so well together."

Jade bit down hard on her bottom lip and held still. She was a quiet woman, a reserved, controlled woman. Never before had she given in to raw sexual need.

"Are you awake?" Byron said when she'd been silent a long time.

"Yes," she said quietly.

He raised his head to see her face. "Are you okay?"

She nodded.

Byron eased aside, rolled to his back, and drew her on top of him. "Tell me what you're thinking."

"I thought knowing what people think was your business."

"Ah." With one large, long-fingered hand, he cradled her face into the hollow of his shoulder. "This is going to be a problem."

"What is?" He was big and lithe and solid—and for this moment he made her feel he could hold away the world.

"Your perception of me versus what I am. You

said you were just an ordinary woman, love. I'm just an ordinary man. And what I'm feeling for you is very special. Can that be enough for you for now?"

She didn't understand what he was asking. "What just happened between us doesn't mean you owe me anything. We both took, Byron." God, what had she done? How would she face him each time she came to work from now on?

"And we both gave. Rest, Jade. Don't think. And let me hold you."

She made her body relax. After several moments, she put an arm around his waist and nestled until she was comfortable.

"You feel so good," Byron murmured. He grabbed the quilt and hauled it over them. "I don't know about you, but it's fine with me if the world stops right here."

"Mm."

"Does that mean you wouldn't mind either?"

"It means . . . Byron, I've never done anything impetuous before—not like this."

"I believe you." He combed her hair with his fingers. "Maybe you'd consider doing it again sometimes?"

She stiffened and tried to pull away. Byron held her fast. "This was . . . I don't want to say this was a mistake," she told him. "But it wasn't rational."

"You didn't enjoy it?"

She squeezed her eyes shut. "You're never going to know how much I enjoyed it. But it can't happen again. Not if my life is going to stay in one piece."

"I don't understand."

"Of course you don't. You're here for a vacation—and to write or whatever you're doing. Then you'll return to California. You won't be thinking about a woman you . . . had sex with in a Cornish village. And that's the way it should be. Maybe I can do the same thing in my own way."

"Why shouldn't you?"

She felt slightly sick. "I can. And I will. But not if I come here each day and find you waiting to take me to bed." He wasn't denying that she classified as a casual encounter.

"I didn't have any plans to take advantage of you, Jade."

"I've got to go." Sitting up, she swung her legs over the side of the bed, and remembered she was naked. "Please look the other way."

"Why?" He sounded amazed.

"Because I'm embarrassed, that's why. I'm not used to walking around in front of a man like this."

"I know you're not."

She faced him. "*How* do you know? What makes you think you're the only man who'd be interested in me?"

His hand shot out so fast she had no time to evade his fingers. "Jade Perron. No man could look at you and not want you. And no man could look at you, then get to know you even a little, and not want you again and again. I'm in the latter category."

Her arm was firmly clasped and he began to pull her toward him. "Thank you," she said. "I think. But that's exactly what I'm afraid of. I've got a job to do here. And I've got to get it finished in a reasonable length of time."

"How long is reasonable?" His gaze centered on

her mouth and his lips parted as he leaned closer. "One month? Two? Six?"

"Let me go, Byron. This is serious."

"It most certainly is." He kissed her, gently pulled her bottom lip between his teeth. And while he grazed and nibbled the already tender skin, he used his free hand to smooth a path over her hip and waist, up her ribs, and finally to her breast. Her nipple sprang instantly to rigid sensitivity and Byron chuckled against her mouth. "You are a very sexy lady."

"Enough!"

Springing away, Jade shot from the bed and rushed around to retrieve her clothes.

Byron watched her every move. "Could I recommend a nice, hot shower before you dig into your plastering or painting or whatever? You may find you've used a few muscles that were rusty. Hot water would take the ache away."

With her fragile underwear in one hand, she glowered at him. "You're so sure of yourself, aren't you? What makes you think any of my muscles would be sore just because . . . Well, just . . . Well . . ."

"Well, just because I know, that's why. And I'm into civilized behavior. So, like the gentleman I am, I'm going to go downstairs and whip up some coffee and juice and eggs and toast and whatever else I can find while you take that shower in peace."

He got out of bed and Jade quickly overcame her natural inclination to look away. Smiling at her, he moved with confident grace to pull a pair of jeans from a closet. These he stepped into. To Jade he tossed one of his shirts.

"What's this for?"

"For you. Why not be comfortable while you eat? Pretend we're on an extended, romantic weekend. Lovers doing the things lovers do."

"We're not—"

"I know that. Why not do it anyway? Then I'll leave you alone and you can go back to work." He was already heading out the door. "And if it's what you want, we'll forget this morning ever happened."

Within twenty minutes, showered, wearing her silk underwear beneath Byron's crisp, long cotton shirt, Jade padded barefoot into the kitchen.

"Dog!" she said, scandalized. "*What* are you doing?" Dog appeared to be eating the best cut of prime rib from a Wedgewood dish.

"Uh, uh, uh," Byron admonished, slathering butter on toast that looked more than slightly overdone. "No talking to my champion that way. My friend, Dog, deserves the best of everything. She has demonstrated the depth of her concern for my well-being and I intend to pay her back."

Jade had to smile. She passed Byron and removed the pot from the coffee maker. He'd put two mugs on the table and she filled them, sniffing appreciatively as she did so.

"The eggs didn't work out," Byron said. "I think I'm out of practice."

Jade replaced the coffeepot. "Television personalities probably don't get much opportunity to cook their own eggs."

He became still. "So I have been noticed—other than as a potential child molester."

"I'm sorry about that. But I don't . . . I didn't know you and I was worried about Ian."

"Your cousin," he said in an oddly constrained voice. "Somehow it's hard for me to imagine that. Will he be able to come and visit?"

"Why do you want him to?" With cream and sugar, she returned to the table.

"Like you, I'm fond of kids and he seems special. Does there have to be more reason than that?"

"You don't have any kids of your own?"

The toast he'd been carrying almost fell from the plate. He caught it just in time. "I told you I'm a widower."

"Widowers sometimes have children."

He put the plate on the table. "Intimacy really scares you. You want it—I can see that in you, feel it in you. But something happened to make you wary. Somebody must have hurt you. Who hurt you, Jade? Who made you afraid to risk getting involved with another man?"

"My husband."

He stopped, his head bowed. "Mr. Perron?"

"Mr. Perron is my father. I already told you that. I was married to a man called Doug Lyman. It didn't pan out."

She could have sworn he sighed. "Do you want to talk about that?"

"No."

"Uh-huh. That was pretty definite. Was he the son in Perron and Son? As in son-in-law?"

"No. The son is my brother, Peter."

"I see. So Peter works in the business, too."

"No. Can we drop this subject?"

Byron looked back at her. "Which one? Doug Lyman, or your brother?"

"Both. I'll talk to Aunt Muriel and see if she'll agree to let me bring Ian over."

"You will?" He straightened and smiled. "That would be great."

"What will you charge for the lessons?"

Byron frowned. "Lessons?"

"The guitar lessons. I'm going to pay for them."

A swatch of red spread over each of his cheekbones. "You won't be paying me for anything. No one will. What I do for Ian, I'll do because he's my . . . Sometimes it's good just to do something because it makes you feel good."

"But we can't—"

He grabbed her, silencing what she'd intended to say, and swung her in front of him. Bending her backward, Byron kissed her, and kissed her until she clawed his shoulders and wrenched her face away.

"You are so beautiful." He looked at her and there was no gentleness in that look. "I want you, Jade."

"No." She shook her head. "We can't do this."

"We already did. Now I want to do it again."

Her head told her that if she didn't stop him, the next weeks would be impossible.

"Give me this, Jade. Please." The green of his eyes turned dark and intense. His lips parted and he anchored her with an arm behind her back. "Will you?"

She said nothing. But neither did she make any attempt to stop him.

Shirt buttons flew and scattered on the floor. Byron sat on the edge of the kitchen table and hiked her up to sit astride his hips. He kissed her until she moaned, and worked the cups of her bra beneath her breasts until he could roll her still-tender nipples between fingers and thumbs.

"Kiss me," he ordered. A pulse at his temple throbbed visibly.

Jade kissed him, putting all the force of her own need into the taking of his mouth.

For a moment, he set her on the floor once more and she heard his zipper part. He didn't bother to remove his jeans, or her panties.

What Byron Frazer wanted, and what Jade Perron needed, was easily accomplished. He thrust her down upon him, filled her, took and gave back.

In the warm kitchen, closed in by gray fog that closed out the day, Jade wrapped her legs around Byron's waist.

It was too late to go back.

Chapter Eleven

"Shirley told me I could come up," Doug Lyman told Jade. "Why wouldn't she?"

This was absolutely the last thing she could face today. "Why *would* she? We both know I've asked you not to come here."

Blond, brown-eyed, with the same appealingly innocent air he'd had when he and Jade had been in school together, Doug spread his calloused, fisherman's hands and raised big shoulders inside one of the navy blue Guernsey sweaters she'd once found solid and comforting.

"I didn't come to argue, Jay. We've known each other a long time and—"

"Don't." She shook her head and returned to stabbing the wire-like stems of a fresh delivery of sweet Williams into a vase with a too-narrow neck.

"Come on, Jay." Doug held a black belt in wheedling. "Why keep on carrying a grudge? It's Sunday morning. The sun's shining—"

"And I suppose you just came from church and one of Reverend Alvaston's rousing sermons on brotherly love."

"*Brotherly* love wasn't what I had in mind."

Jade shot upright.

Doug actually looked abashed. "Sorry. I shouldn't have said that. You make it hard for a man to keep his mind off . . . well, we both know how I feel about you."

If she were to spend the rest of her life analyzing Doug Lyman—and she didn't intend to spend even a moment on the project if she could help it—but if she did, Jade would never comprehend the man's incredible nerve.

"Anyway," he continued. "It's such a great day I thought, why not try again? You're worth it, Jade. I'd come crawling as many times as it took if we could put the past behind us, you know that."

Jade glanced at the door—foolishly left open earlier when she carried in the vacuum stored in a cupboard at the top of the stairs. Doug had simply climbed those stairs and walked in, smiling and trying to do what he'd once done so successfully: convince her that, for him, she was the only woman who could ever truly be important.

"Where's Rose?"

Doug's smile wavered. "Downstairs with Shirley."

"Oh." Jade crossed her arms and sat on the edge of a chair. "So that's how you did it."

"You always were so suspicious. Can't you try—"

"No. I can't try anything where you're concerned. You know Shirley putters around in the shop on Sundays. And you know Shirley's a sucker for children. Particularly very sweet little children, like Rose. So you used your own daughter as a diversionary tactic. You knew Shirley wouldn't turn Rose away—"

"Jade—"

"You sure as hell knew she'd turn *you* away."

"I need you."

She felt suddenly, deeply sick. "Don't let yourself do this, Doug. You need *someone*, you don't need me. Once I hated you enough to wish for a moment like this. Now I don't hate you, I don't feel anything for you—except embarrassment that you'd make such a fool of yourself."

"When did you learn to be such a bitch?"

"Get out." She stood up and her knee collided with the yellow chest forcefully enough to rattle her collection of lacquered boxes. "Go now. Be good to Rose, Doug, and be grateful God gave you someone so special who'll love you regardless of what you are. I love her, too. She's important to me because she's Rose, and because you've made sure she's important to me. I want to be here for her when I can, but I'd be happy never to see your face again."

"I said I need you, dammit." He approached but Jade felt no threat. Doug might be a basic louse but he was a gentle, basic louse. He said, "This last year has been hell. I bought the new boat and I don't have to tell you the runs have been down—way down. You know how tight money is right now. I can't get the kind of loan I need to tide me over."

Slowly and heavily, her shoulders relaxed. He would always manage to shock her. "You came to ask me to lend you money?"

"No!" He reached for her, but Jade drew back. "I'm here to ask you to . . . Give me another chance, Jay. I need you, and Rose needs you. You've just admitted it. We both need a family and you're the only one who can give us that."

"This is unbelievable!"

"Don't shout. Shirley might hear. And Rose."

"I'm not shouting. We're finished. We were finished years ago when you decided to have an affair." She wouldn't mention names. Names made it all too real again.

"A partnership is what I'm suggesting," Doug said. "Yes, I want more than a business relationship with you, and I think that'll come in time. But Art never appreciated you like he should. I'm going to give you the opportunity to become part of something that'll really be yours."

Jade studied him, uncomprehending.

"I'm going to have my own canning business one day. Lyman's will be a name that's known all over the country for canned fish. All I need is the capital—enough to get me caught up—and I'll never look back. Diversification is what counts. I've got the ideas, Jade, and you've got the money."

"You're talking about a small fortune," she said slowly.

"Don't tell me you haven't salted away a small fortune in the past few years," he said, his lips thinning.

"Since you got out of my life and stopped taking every penny that was mine for your own? Is that what you mean?"

"A wife's possessions are her husband's." His voice rose a notch. "What was yours belonged to me by right. I married you."

"My God." She could scarcely concentrate. "*You* married me? Thank you so very much. A wife's possessions are her husband's? Doug, we're out of the bloody Middle Ages, in case you haven't noticed. Go away and leave me alone. The answer is *no*. It will always be *no!*"

"It's always been good enough for your mother to let your father wear the trousers." He came a step closer. "And you've worked since you were eighteen for a man who made a partner of your brother—*when your brother doesn't even work in the business and you do*. I'm offering you a chance to *share*, Jade. I'll look after you and your name will be the one over the door."

"My name," she said softly. "You mean Perron? Jade Perron?"

He stared. "Don't be daft. You know I'm asking you to marry me again. Lyman's the name. Lyman would *be* the name. Doug Lyman. If we're married, it'll be your name, too, won't it?"

NEW TO YOU.

Byron stood on the opposite side of the narrow street and read, and reread, the red script sign over the shop with double display windows and a central door also painted red. A card wedged in the corner of one window announced that the shop was closed.

Another door stood to the left of the shop, and another to the right. Small metal crates containing empty milk bottles glinted dully in the afternoon sun.

With his hands in the pockets of his jeans, Byron crossed the road and approached the door on the left side of New to You. A name had been written on a minute piece of card and inserted into a brass-rimmed slot below the bell. Patting his jacket in search of glasses, he peered and read:

Trevay. By the time he reached the other door, he'd located and donned the glasses. *Hill*. He considered. Yes, Jade had said she rented her flat from a woman named Hill.

Damn it all, anyway! Ian was his reason for being here and he was going to spend some time with him. He was almost sure Jade would find a way to bring him together with the boy. Even if the decision about Ian's future was Byron's to make—which it legally was not—he couldn't make that decision without weighing all the potential outcomes. It could be that helping Ian to be happier where he was would be right. It could be that stepping over a very dangerous line and telling him who he was would be more confusion than an already uprooted thirteen-year-old could take.

An image of his own father came to mind. Byron shut the man out. He was not part of who his son had become. It would be great not to remember anything about a childhood filled with people who left you. Always leaving. All the ones he'd loved, or wanted to love, always leaving him.

A victim by default, and never able to fight back because he couldn't fight someone, or for someone who wasn't around anymore.

His own history was being repeated in Ian's life, but it didn't have to keep on being repeated.

Byron turned his back on the shop and pushed the glasses, which fuzzed his distance vision, hard against the bridge of his nose. Yesterday had been heaven. And it had been hell. He'd argued for a day off, pointed out that it was Saturday. Jade had flatly told him that she couldn't afford the luxury of lazy Saturdays. They'd both attempted to work. Finally, when it had become obvious that neither of them would get anything done as long as they remained in the same space, Byron had left. When he returned—by the nine o'clock and last ferry—she'd gone.

They had to talk.

What exactly did he hope to say, and to accomplish?

Yesterday should be classified as a mistake, but who could classify such a . . . Not a mistake, just a potential disaster, a wonderful potential disaster that *had* to be handled with extreme care.

He had hurt Jade.

Byron slipped off his glasses, folded them, and turned back to the shop. His life was dedicated to mending people, not hurting them. And Jade was one of the last people he could bear to wound.

The shop door was whipped open to reveal a dun-colored woman: dun-colored braids, pale dun-colored skin, dun-colored clothes of some cotton stuff, the loose skirts of which brushed the tops of dun-colored feet in brown sandals.

"Morning." She smiled and he realized her eyes were a very pleasant shade of golden brown. "No. Afternoon. Sorry about that."

"Hi. I'm looking for—"

"You're Byron Frazer."

Even in the States, the average citizen on the street didn't recognize him. "Yes."

"Behavioral psychologist. American. Personality on the telly."

"I do appear on television."

"You don't like to be called a TV personality?"

"It always suggests a talk-show host—or maybe an evangelist. That's not really the image I hope to project."

"I suppose that's important in your line of work? Image?"

He probably should ask who she was. "Trust is probably the issue more than image."

She seemed to consider that. "Doesn't fit," she said in a preoccupied tone.

"I beg your pardon."

"I don't very often make mistakes. Of course, I hadn't met you. Have you suffered a great deal from the jealousy of others?"

Byron experienced a rare and total blank.

"A leader," the woman said. "Yes, of course. And easily upset and excitable. Very concerned with the opinions others form of you."

He collected himself. "This is all very interesting. Are you, by any chance, Miss Hill?"

"Mrs. Hill." Her eyes cleared. "Shirley to my friends, and you qualify. I expect you're looking for Jade."

He experienced an odd discomfort which quickly perished. In this town, everyone knew everyone else. He'd already discovered that his presence had been noted. No doubt it was also common knowledge that Jade Perron was working at Ferryneath.

"Did you want to see Jade?" Shirley thrust her chin forward inquiringly.

"Well—yes." Jade had left him in no doubt that she would not appreciate any suggestion of a personal relationship between them. "I want to talk to her about the cottage. Is she in, perhaps?"

Shirley sighed hugely. "Oh, yes. Very rarely anywhere else unless she's working. It's about time that girl had herself some fun, Dr. Frazer."

"Byron."

"Byron. Jade's very beautiful, you know."

He barely stopped himself from effusive agreement. "An attractive woman, yes."

Shirley Hill's brown eyes became sharp. "Yes, well. Go on through the shop and into the storeroom at the back. You'll find Jade upstairs."

"Thank you." He waited for her to stand aside, then passed into the shop's dim interior. "Interesting business. Different stock all the time, I suppose."

Shirley closed the door again. "Everything in this shop has a story to tell," she said seriously. "Some of them have many."

Byron murmured concurrence and moved on purposefully to the back of the showroom.

"Was this an impulse?" Shirley said.

"An impulse?" He'd entered a windowless room crammed with boxes of every shape and size.

"Picking up and leaving the States? Coming here? Did you get a sudden urge to get away from your surroundings and examine your soul in a distant land?"

He opened his mouth to say no. "Ah . . . Yes, in a way. Yes, I suppose you could say that." A lucky guess on her part, but he couldn't deny that she'd come close to the truth. "Thank you for letting me in." She didn't exhibit signs of substance abuse— at least none that he'd noted.

Partway up the stairs, Byron paused. From above came the sound of a man's rumbling voice. He leaned against the wall and felt foolish. There had been an instant, vaguely jealous and decidedly possessive flare in response to those masculine tones.

He had no right to feel possessive of Jade Perron.

But he did.

Jade had a father and a brother and probably other relatives and friends who didn't qualify as romantic interests. Hell! He knew better than anyone that she hadn't been close—not *close* close to a man in a long time.

How did he know?

He just did. And anyway, she'd said as much. Would she be embarrassed by his arrival?

A contrary burst of determination propelled Byron upward. He intended to spend a lot more time with Jade. She could try to resist him, but he could be one very determined man. No, he didn't know where it would lead and, yes, he acknowledged it might be a long time before they . . . If he didn't cool it, she'd probably find a way to avoid him altogether and that wasn't what he wanted. He wanted to at least find out what he wanted.

And he wanted her to trust him enough to bring Ian to Ferryneath. For now he refused to address the potential problems presented by her relationship by adoption to Ian Spring, or by whatever her reaction might be to discovering what had brought Byron to England in the first place.

At the top of the stairs was a short hallway. A door with two pebbled-glass panels stood ajar at the other end. His tennis shoes making no sound, Byron walked on.

"You spoil her, Jade," the male voice said. "Five-year-old girls don't need a pound to spend on sweets."

Reminding himself that Shirley Hill had told

him to go ahead and see Jade, Byron tapped a glass panel.

"Come in, Shirley," Jade said.

Byron pushed open the door. "Not Shirley, I'm afraid. Hi, Jade. Is it okay if I come in?" Even as he spoke, he advanced into a room the color of the sunshine outside.

Jade wore a red scarf over her hair. The tails of a red-and-white-checked shirt were tied in front—exposing several inches of smooth, bare midriff above tight, oft-washed jeans. Her feet were bare and a vacuum parked near a rattan chair covered with yellow cushions suggested Sunday was house-work day.

She looked absolutely wonderful.

He'd like to pull her into his arms right now . . . and that was only the beginning of what he'd like.

She also looked as if someone had just dropped ice down her back.

Byron smiled engagingly and turned his attention to the room's other occupants. A tall, broad-shouldered man with blond hair stood there. He held Rose's hand. Rose looked at Byron and raised her shoulders to her ears. She grinned, showing a gap in her teeth, and glowed as if seeing him was a special treat. Then she looked from Jade to the man, and pure, innocent delight lit her eyes. In the palm of her free hand she displayed a shiny pound coin.

The child eyed her prize and then checked for Byron's reaction. He made suitably round and ap-proving eyes, and said, "Hi, there, Rose. Lucky you."

The man promptly pulled the child closer and settled a protective hand on her mop of curly black hair. His expression sent only one message. He hated Byron on sight.

"Hi. I'm Byron Frazer." He shot out a hand, which the man eventually held and instantly released. "I came to have a few words with Jade."

"What about?" The tone matched the glare.

Some men could smile and acknowledge the potential for hate at the same time. Byron smiled. "It's personal." He kept his voice soft, his engaging grin in place.

"Jade doesn't have any secrets—"

"Doug!" She appeared to have just remembered she was alive. "Doug, thanks for bringing Rose by. Good luck with . . . Well, good luck."

"I'm Doug Lyman," the man said.

The ex-husband. "Good to meet you." Even honest men sometimes lied in the name of civilized behavior.

"You're over at Ferryneath."

He barely smothered a groan. "So much for peace and anonymity in a quaint Cornish town. I'm staying at Ferryneath, yes."

"That was something else I wanted to talk to you about," Lyman said to Jade. "Word has it you're working over there on your own."

"I almost always work alone." She played with the lapel of her shirt.

"You need to look out for things like that," Lyman said. "Working alone in a house with a man. I don't like it."

Byron watched Jade's face turn even paler than usual. She inclined her head toward Rose. "This isn't the time, Doug. Please be careful on the stairs."

"What's he here for?" Lyman spoke as if Byron

were deaf . . . or dead. "People are already talking."

He heard a snapping sound and saw a flower stem fracture between Jade's fingers. Coming had been a bad idea.

Jade walked behind Doug Lyman and opened the door wide. "You watch how you go, Rose. Daddys can be clumsy sometimes."

Lyman stared at Byron. For the first time in his life he knew he was confronted by a man who had picked him out as a threat to his relationship with a woman.

Divorced or not, Doug Lyman still regarded Jade as his.

"Can we go to buy sweeties, Daddys?" the child asked.

Jade stooped quickly and hugged Rose. "Don't you spend all that on sweeties at once, snippet. You'll get a tummyache."

Lyman collected himself and turned his attention to his daughter. "Daddy will take care of his girl, won't he, pet? We'll go and buy some of those Smarties© you like. How would you like it if we put the change in your pig? Then we can pop up the sweet shop lots of times."

Rose nodded. "Can we have chips with our dinner?"

"Chips with dinner, it is." Without another word, Lyman led the girl from the room and down the stairs.

When the sound of their footsteps had entirely faded, Jade flopped onto the couch, rested her head back, and closed her eyes.

"Mr. Lyman wasn't pleased to see me," Byron

said. The tense set of her face loaded him with guilt. "Does that matter?"

"You shouldn't have come here."

He spread his feet. "I asked if it mattered that your ex-husband disliked seeing another man visit you."

Her eyes opened. "What does or doesn't matter to me," she said in an even voice that didn't fool him into a second of comfort, "is none of your business. Anything about me is none of your business. It's none of anyone's business but mine."

"True," he said. "Sorry. Rose is such a little sweetheart."

"She is." Jade's expression became closed.

Byron thought about the child, about her dark curly hair and pale skin, and screwed up his eyes. "Five, you said."

"No, I didn't say. You must have overheard."

Jade had been divorced more than five years. "She has her father's eyes." The timing of her divorce didn't have to mean a thing.

"Mm."

But where did the black curls and pale skin come from? Byron discarded his line of thought. Jade wasn't the only woman with that coloring.

"Does Lyman's wife approve of him behaving like a possessive husband with you?"

Her stare made him wish he'd kept his mouth shut.

"Doug doesn't have a wife."

He could just come out and ask if Rose was her daughter. No, he couldn't. And whether she was or wasn't had nothing to do with Byron's involvement with Jade.

"I'm going to arrange for someone else to finish Ferryneath," Jade said.

His heart did something decidedly nasty—and so did his stomach. "Why?"

Jade pushed to the edge of the couch and stood up. She advanced upon him until they stood close enough for Byron to see the fascinating violet halos around the pupils of her eyes.

"I'm not playing any more games with you, Byron."

"Have we been playing games? Is that what we did?"

"You heard what I said. No games. What you're doing now is definitely a form of game playing. You ask me why I'm getting someone else to work at Ferryneath and I'm supposed to say you know why. Then you'll say 'Trust me,' or something equally original, and I'll be supposed to solemnly ask if you think you can trust yourself—or maybe I'm supposed to say I'm not sure I can trust *myself*. And so the game goes on until you get what you want."

"Do you trust yourself?"

"Yes." She dragged the scarf from her hair. "Of course I do."

"Then what's the problem? I didn't rape you, Jade."

"Oh." Her throat moved convulsively. "I . . . What a horrible thing to say. You were the one who started what happened."

"I never forced you."

She pressed the scarf to her mouth and shook her head.

Byron knew a moment's utter self-disgust. "But I

did start it, Jade. You're right. Please don't . . . Don't feel badly about what we did. That's why I came, to tell you I wouldn't change a thing about being with you, except knowing that you were going to have a hard time with it afterwards."

"I don't want to talk about this."

He knew he mustn't try to touch her. "Okay. We won't, only please don't cut off something that might bring us both a lot of happiness."

"Happiness?" Her eyes glistened with tears. "I enjoyed being with you. I'm not going to pretend I didn't. But I'm not the kind of woman who goes to bed with a man she hardly knows. I shouldn't have done that."

She didn't have to tell him how much she'd enjoyed him, and herself *with* him. "We didn't just go to bed, as you put it," he reminded her. "Sweetheart, you and I made spectacular love in more places than bed."

Jade covered her ears. *"Don't* say that."

He did reach for her then, and she whirled away.

"Okay. For a man who makes his living saying the right things, or trying to say the right things, I'm making a hash of this. I came to tell you I don't regret making love yesterday, but I do regret that as a result of what I caused, you feel in an untenable position." And now he sounded like a legal argument. "You have my word that I won't put a finger on you again if you don't invite me to do so, Jade. Please carry on with the job you've started. If you suddenly insist on turning it over to someone else, you may do exactly what you don't want to do."

"Which is?" She raised her chin in a defiant gesture that made Byron feel better.

"You could cause more rumors of the kind your husband mentioned."

"*Ex*-husband," she said with enough vehemence to bring Byron a real surge of good cheer. "And I don't give a damn what people say about me."

"I doubt that. Anyway, there's nothing to fear from good old, well-behaved Byron anymore. The other reason I came was to ask if you could arrange with Miss Cadwen for Ian to come over after school tomorrow. He called me and sounded pretty down." And Byron had barely contained himself from rushing over to Muriel Cadwen's house to claim his son. Then sanity had returned and he acknowledged he had no right to do any such thing . . . yet.

"It won't work," Jade said.

"Yes it will. The boy needs to be around a man who understands the things that interest him." Even without the obligation Byron felt, he was very qualified to know what the lack of caring male influence could do to a boy.

"I wasn't talking about Ian. It won't work for you and me to try pretending yesterday never happened."

"I don't have any intention of pretending it didn't happen." He would not lie to Jade. "Wonderful things don't happen often enough and I'm not about to toss one aside. But I've got plenty of willpower. It's something I've had to have in my life. Like I already told you, we won't make love again until you let me know it's what you want."

"Until?"

"Okay, unless. Is that better? Is it okay?" He bowed, bringing his face a little closer. "I'm a trustworthy man. If you don't believe me, you can get plenty of references."

"You make it sound as if it's only a matter of time before . . . You talk as if we will be lovers again when I come to my senses."

He grinned. "Something like that. But I also admit I've been known to be wrong. At least, I probably was once."

She let him coax a smile from her. "I don't think I should work at the cottage again."

"I do."

"I don't."

"My sexual magnetism is so strong you won't be able to resist me? Understandable."

She cocked her head. Her hair was tied in a ponytail, leaving her vulnerably slender neck very exposed. Byron's eyes fell to the dip behind her left collarbone, where the shirt lapel lay open to a trace of bra strap—red bra strap. He swallowed.

"Can we give it another try? With you working at Ferryneath, I mean?" Byron used his best, reasonable tone.

"I'm not sure. What if the try fails?"

A stimulating thought. "We won't let it. Please, Jade. I'm going to feel so responsible if you have to change plans you made a year ago."

She slipped the splayed fingers of one hand inside the neck of her blouse.

Byron followed the gesture and remembered her breasts, naked in the silver light of a foggy morning, dusky, uptilted nipples springing hard from such silken, white skin.

"I think you should go and speak to Aunt Muriel yourself."

Byron blinked and met her eyes. "Why would I do that?"

"Because she's Ian's legal guardian and she's the one to make decisions about him."

"Jade." *He must not touch her.* "I'll be happy to go to Miss Cadwen if you'll come with me."

She crouched to stroke Dog, who had slept throughout on a braided rug before the empty fireplace. "You don't need me, or anyone, Byron. You're a very self-assured man."

He could correct her. He could say that he was a very self-assured man on the outside and to some extent on the inside—but only to some extent. "Will you come anyway?"

For a moment he thought she'd refuse. But she dropped to sit cross-legged beside Dog and sent Byron a wry look. "You are very persuasive, Byron Frazer. No wonder you're such a success as a psychologist. All right. I'll come with you to Aunt Muriel's."

"Tomorrow?"

"Well—"

"Ian really sounded needy."

"Aunt Muriel is a kind woman." There was more than a hint of defensiveness in Jade's voice. "She's doing the best she can. There has to be a time of adjustment—for both of them."

"Of course. You're absolutely right. But tomorrow will work for you? We can go over on the ferry together and bring him back." He didn't miss the pursing of her lips. "I'll probably be out a good deal of the day—while you're working—but I'll get back in time to come over to Fowey. Then I'll be busy with Ian and you can get on with things again."

"I ought to refuse."

"But you won't."

"I . . . won't." Jade bounced to her feet. "I'll see how it goes, Byron. But I meant it about . . . Well, I meant what I said."

"So did I." And he remembered what he'd said, and what he hadn't exactly said. He didn't want to leave her now, but she showed no sign of encouraging him to stay. "I'd better let you get back to whatever you were doing, then?"

"Yes. Is Shirley still in the shop?"

Byron shook his head. "I don't know."

"I'll see you out and lock the door."

He followed her downstairs, searching for some way to prolong the visit.

Shirley Hill's face, popping into the storeroom, squelched any hope of inspiration. "There you are," she said. "Sorry about Doug, Jade. Rose is such a little darling and—"

"And we both love kiddies," Jade told her. "Don't be sorry. Doug isn't a problem."

Something in the exchange brought Byron satisfaction. Doug Lyman wasn't a popular visitor in these parts.

"Are you going out?" Hope shimmered in Shirley's eyes and in her trilled words. "Ready-money Cove is lovely on a day like this."

"The dust in my flat isn't lovely on a day like this," Jade said. "And I'm sure Dr. Frazer has things he needs to attend to."

The dismissal was there. He wouldn't push again today. Jade saw him to the door and stood there, her arms wrapped around her bare middle, as he stepped onto the sidewalk.

"Enjoy your dusting," he told her.

"I will."

"I'll see you tomorrow, then?" he risked asking.

"Yes."

He looked at her and couldn't manage a smile. "Goodbye, Jade."

"Yes."

Shirley's face appeared yet again, this time from behind Jade's head. "Byron," she said, sounding breathless. "When's your birthday?"

He glanced at Jade, who gave no hint as to how he should react. "November second. Why?"

Shirley let out a shriek of delighted laughter. "I was right in the first place. Toodles, Byron." Dismissing him, she began to pull Jade back into the shop. "This is perfect. What did I tell you? Ooh, exactly right. Dark. Deep. Black and red. They thrive on passion. But you've got to watch out for anger, mind you. The temper can be a challenge. Willful, very willful. That often needs taking under control."

The last word that Byron heard before the door shut was ". . . Scorpio."

her arms wrapped around her bare shoulders as he
stepped onto the sidewalk.

"I know you don't me," he told her.

"Troll."

"It's me, your Santhony doing," he raised saying

He looked at Bett and credit, managed a smile.
"Cookies, Julie."

Slowly the repeated color again a question
think, Julie said. "No one," one said, studying
his face. "Who's your brother?"

He stared at Bett, the eyes told her with may
his brother eyes. Remember around. "Who"
was light in the dim place. For days, Bruno, DR
he stood there, she began hand.l park back into the
there. "She's Bruno. What, and I tell your brot
written right, until Bruno. Here, and now, they
there in prison but will let you to stand on the
you can't mind you. The trip to can be a sentence
written way what. That chern bread took its light
second.

The last word was, Bruno Bruno. Before, the
floor still was, to soothe.

Chapter Twelve

Like two honor guards, china dalmatians flanked an oak case clock on the high mantel in Aunt Muriel's parlor.

The only sound in the room, the clock's ticking grew louder and louder, or so it seemed to Jade.

She watched the brass second hand flick rhythmically on its way around the steel face.

Aunt Muriel sighed loudly, and from the corner of her eye, Jade saw her aunt uncross her sensible brown brogues and recross them in the opposite direction.

Outside, the temperature had climbed close to seventy degrees, but a dispirited fire stroked flames over the blackened firebox.

Byron coughed. He sat beside Jade on an overstuffed couch covered with dark green crushed velvet splotched with brown peonies.

At Jade's suggestion they'd arrived early at the terrace house in Fowey. Her idea had been to deal with any awkwardness between Aunt Muriel and Byron before Ian got home. So much for careful plans.

"Nice clock," Byron said.

Jade stuffed down the laugh that rose in her throat.

"Thank you," Aunt Muriel said. "They gave it to me when I retired . . . from the library."

Silence slithered in to settle between the ticking once more.

"Will you have more tea?" Aunt Muriel asked.

"No, thank you," Byron and Jade responded in unison, and laughed uncomfortably.

"Your hanging baskets are great," Byron said.

"In front?" Aunt Muriel, kept her eyes on folded hands in her lap.

"Yes," Byron said. "The begonias are . . . they're really something. You must have a green thumb. And your roses are wonderful. Very therapeutic, gardening. Many of my patients take it up."

Jade caught her bottom lip between her teeth and stole a glance at Aunt Muriel, who didn't "hold" with people telling their "personal trials" to strangers. To Aunt Muriel, all members of the psychiatric community were classified as strangers.

"It certainly is a comfort to me," Aunt Muriel said, shocking Jade with the first deviation from expected behavior she ever remembered in this woman. "I expect you deal with a lot of troubled souls. Sort of like a minister, aren't you?"

Jade's mouth twitched. This time she looked at Byron. "Is that how your patients view you, Byron? As a spiritual leader?"

He did not appear amused. "Your aunt's choice of words was quite appropriate. My job is to minister to people—to families—who feel they've gotten a bit lost. Or to people who've found parts of themselves they thought they'd lost and who don't like what they've been forced to look at. What time will Ian be home, Miss Cadwen?"

She raised her arched red brows even closer to her hairline and checked the clock. "He's usually here by three-thirty at the latest." There was another sigh. "But you can never tell. He hasn't had a lot of guidance, Dr. Frazer. Ada, my dear departed sister, was a gentle woman. Soft, some might say, but I always thought of Ada as having a deep strength. Anyway, she was widowed a few years back and I can only think she let the boy run wild. He just doesn't understand the things a nice English boy understands by the time he's thirteen."

"He does know we're coming?" Byron said.

Aunt Muriel leaned over the arm of her chair and rummaged for something Jade couldn't see.

"I don't hold with getting children excited," she said, surfacing with a large skein of peachy orange wool, a pair of knitting needles, and part of a garment. "Best not let them spend too much time thinking about things, if you know what I mean."

"You didn't tell him we were coming."

"No." Aunt Muriel consulted a dog-eared knitting pattern for several seconds before driving a needle ferociously through a loop and springing into rapid action.

In the ensuing seconds, the nerve-destroying squidge, squidge of nylon-covered metal obliterated the clock's ticking.

Jade glanced around at the high sideboard with its long, embroidered white runner, at the chairs that matched the sofa upon which she and Byron sat, at an ancient player piano in a recess beside the fireplace, and finally, at a drop-leaf table buttressing one wall. Showcased on the table was a pink glass bowl filled with plastic fruit.

Over all hung the aroma of old dust anchored to wooden surfaces with lavender wax.

Byron shifted forward on the couch. "I do want you to understand that I believe it may do Ian some good to spend time with a fellow American."

The needles stilled. "Ian's English now, or he will be just as soon as we can arrange to have him naturalized."

White formed along Byron's clenching knuckles, startling Jade. "Ian's decided he wants to take British citizenship?" Byron asked.

Something in his tone grabbed Jade's attention. She watched him covertly, noting a small twitch in the muscle beside his mouth and the tension in his compressed lips.

"Some things have to be decided for children until they're old enough to decide for themselves. When Ian's twenty-one, he can do as he pleases. Of course, by then he'll be proud to have embraced his mother's country."

"What about his father's country?" Byron's mild delivery didn't deceive Jade. There was something here that troubled him deeply.

"He doesn't have a father anymore," Muriel said, yanking out yarn from the skein like a fireman about to attack a major blaze.

"No, and I'm sorry both the Springs died." Byron raked his fingers up and down his thighs. "I don't have a father or mother anymore either. That doesn't mean I cease to be an American."

Jade caught Byron's eye and shook her head

slightly. Antagonizing Aunt Muriel wasn't the way to help Ian.

"This is his country now." Aunt Muriel sounded stubborn. "He'll grow up here and go into a trade here and this is where he'll want to owe his allegiance."

"You sound very committed to the boy," Byron said.

"One does what one's duty demands."

"Even if the duty is onerous?"

Aunt Muriel clicked away with freshened fury. "Ian's a good enough boy. And he was my sister's. She loved him and it's my responsibility to love him, too."

Jade's eyes stung. Byron Frazer wouldn't understand, but this woman, with her clumsy, ungracious turn of phrase, had the gentlest heart Jade had ever encountered. Through all Jade's growing years, it had been Aunt Muriel to whom she had turned and Aunt Muriel who somehow managed to fill May Perron's slot without ever criticizing the sister she loved.

"Do American boys do a lot of this guitar playing, then?"

"Playing an instrument's a valuable accomplishment for any boy or girl—or man or woman—regardless of where they come from."

"Mm." Aunt Muriel fished beside her chair once more and pulled aloft a skein of brown yarn. "I always liked my pianola, I must say." She laughed with an unexpectedly young abandon that had the power to make others laugh. "The pianola was my mother's. She gave it to me because she said a girl with ten thumbs might do quite well on the pianola. Ten thumbs and a tin ear."

"You don't like music?"

"I *love* it." Bright blue eyes cast a reproachful glance in Byron's direction. "I can't paint, but that doesn't mean I don't enjoy beautiful pictures. And I can't act, but I'd travel miles to see a good play."

"Point taken." Byron looked at Jade. "Jade has said she'll be responsible for making sure Ian gets home each time he comes. All he'll have to do is get on the ferry. I'll meet him at the other side."

"Why would you go to so much trouble for a boy you don't know?"

Jade, still looking at Byron, saw his eyes fix and become distant. "Let's just say I've always had a nose for need." He gave a short laugh. "And maybe I've got an overdeveloped sense of responsibility, too."

"You're not responsible for Ian. I am."

"Ian's still trying to adjust," Jade said. "It'll make it easier on you if he's got something he likes doing to divert him, Auntie. It's going to mean I can get to know him a bit better, too. He's a member of the family, after all."

"Yes, he is," Aunt Muriel said with a determined pushing back of her shoulders. "One of our own. And we look after our own, don't we, Jade?"

"We certainly do."

"But you think this guitar business will be all right?" Aunt Muriel said. She was much more disturbed than she wanted anyone to know.

"Absolutely," Jade told her. "Byron's very good with young people."

Jade drew in a breath and let it out slowly. How did she know how good Byron was or wasn't with children? She didn't. And she could scarcely believe she was pleading his case.

Why did he want to spend time with Ian?

Were there people who just responded to per-ceived need?

"All right, then," Aunt Muriel said. "If it's all right with you, Jade, then it's all right with me. Ian can go."

"It'll be good for him," Jade heard herself say before the enormity of the situation made itself felt.

She was sitting here, inches from the only man who had made her feel totally female in as long as she could remember, if it had ever happened be-fore at all. Byron had the power to breathe life into her—emotionally and sexually—yet she knew she must keep her distance from him. At the same time she felt at some deep level that he was a kind, good man who wanted to help Ian and who would be a positive influence on him.

Crazy.

"Do you think he'll like this?" Tentativeness had crept into Aunt Muriel's voice. She displayed what was evidently the front of a V-necked sweater. "The colors are nice, don't you think, Dr. Frazer?"

"Oh—very nice," Byron said.

The sweater was a monstrosity, a large version of a child's garment which, even then, would be more appropriate for a girl.

"I thought the little trees in the border were boyish." She fingered a row of small, billowy brown trees that ran along the neck and the hem of the sweater front. "He doesn't have a single hand-knitted jumper. Can you imagine that? I always thought it showed people cared—hand-knitted things. I don't want you to think I blame

Ada, I don't. She must have had her hands full, poor love."

Byron and Jade murmured simultaneously.

The front door slammed.

"There he is now," Muriel said and Jade didn't miss the anticipation in the woman's face and movements. "He'll need to have some tea before he goes."

"He can eat with me," Byron said.

Footsteps went slowly past the parlor door.

"Yoo, hoo!" Aunt Muriel called. "In the parlor, Ian!"

After a pause, the footsteps returned and Ian came into the room.

"Take off your shoes," Aunt Muriel ordered, frowning at Ian's perfectly clean, highly polished black shoes.

He did as he'd been told, but not before he returned Jade's smile and cast a cautiously pleased look at Byron.

"Your cousin Jade, and Dr. Frazer, have been kind enough to take an interest in you. What do you say?"

Ian finished pulling off his shoes and screwed up his eyes. "Thank you?" he said uncertainly.

"I should think so. Come here a minute. I want to hold this up to you."

A bright red flush stole up the boy's neck and over his cheeks. He went obediently to stand before Aunt Muriel.

She tugged him down on his knees and pinned the sweater front to the shoulders of his T-shirt. "Oh, look at that. It's going to be perfect. Oh, I'll see if I can get it done by Sunday so you can wear it to church. Wait till Effie Harding sees it. She'll be

wanting to borrow the pattern to do up for her
son's boy."

Jade got up in a rush. "Look at the time. I've got
to get back to work." And she had to get away from
this painfully embarrassing scene.

"Run along with you, then," Aunt Muriel said,
unpinning Ian. "Don't forget your instrument."

"No, Aunt," Ian said, backing away.

"Tie those shoes properly before you go out. I
don't want you falling over and breaking something."

"No, Aunt."

Aunt Muriel got up and followed the boy into
the hallway with its ivory on ivory flocked paper
above shiny brown-painted wainscotting. "And
mind your manners. Be sure to say thank you to
Dr. Frazer and your cousin Jade."

"I will."

When his shoes were firmly double-knotted and
he stood by the door with Byron and Jade, Aunt
Muriel approached, tutting, and produced a
jacket made of shiny purple nylon with white
sleeves and VIKINGS written across the front in
white. "Put this dreadful thing on," she said, holding it out. "As soon as I can manage it, we'll have to
get you something more suitable. You look like
one of those awful gang members in one of those
American films."

Wordlessly, Ian took the jacket and shrugged it
on.

"That hair needs a good cutting. Effie's girl
does hair cutting at home. Effie says it costs less
than half what they charge in the real shops. I
wouldn't know about these things. I've done my
own for years." She plumped her tight curls with

the palm of a hand. "I suppose I could cut a boy's hair, too."

"Don't you worry, Auntie," Jade said, her stomach turning at the trapped look in Ian's brown eyes. "I'll make sure he gets a haircut. You've got enough to do."

"I'm not complaining about that," Aunt Muriel said. "One does one's duty."

Byron smiled at Aunt Muriel. "You certainly do, Miss Cadwen. More than your duty. You're a very kind woman." He sounded kind, gentle, and Jade's eyes stung yet again.

Aunt Muriel flapped a hand in dismissal, but her pleasure showed.

At last, with Ian ahead, guitar case in hand, Jade fell in beside Byron to walk down the front garden path.

Muriel waved from the doorway. "Watch how you go, mind. And remember what I said about not making a nuisance of yourself."

"I'll bring him back when I come," Jade said, hastening her pace. "Don't worry about him."

"I can't help worrying. Boys and trouble go together. You should hear Effie Harding's stories about her William when he was a youngster. Worries you to death to think about it."

"Ian will be fine, Miss Cadwen," Byron said, his voice far too level.

"Don't stand at the edge on that wretched ferry, mind. There was a boy did that some years back. Fell. Hit his head on the deck on the way and drowned before anyone could get to him."

"He won't stand too close to the edge, Miss Cadwen."